1-900-A-N-Y-T-I-M-E

A Novel

TRACY PRICE-THOMPSON

ATRIA PAPERBACK

New York   London   Toronto   Sydney

ATRIA PAPERBACK

A Division of Simon & Schuster, Inc.
1230 Avenue of the Americas
New York, NY 10020

ATRIA PAPERBACK and colophon are trademarks of
Simon & Schuster, Inc.

Designed by Suet Y. Chong

Manufactured in the United States of America

ISBN 978-1-61523-463-9

This novel is dedicated to the memory of my dear friend, Sandra Jones, who lived with her disabilities with grace and good humor, and who never let her physical limitations stifle her laughter or her passion for the endless pleasures of this world. Sandie will be greatly missed, but her zest for life and the playful twinkle in her eyes will never be forgotten.

For information on birth defects and physical disabilities visit:
National Center on Birth Defects and Developmental Disabilities (NCBDDD) www.cdc.gov/ncbddd.

ACKNOWLEDGMENTS

To Greg, my husband, my best friend, my *Daddy*, my rock. (CIGTL? LOL! That was one!) Daddy, thank you for the gift of your patient and loving companionship and for being the kind of man who readily gets out of bed to bring me nourishment whenever I whisper, "Dear love, I thirst."

God has been good to us, and you have been the bedrock of our family and the most good-natured and giving man in the world. Thank you for ninety-nine (99) years of loving, respecting, and spoiling me as I love, respect, and spoil you in return.

To my children, my babies, the beats of my heart. Thank you for being wonderful young people who have righteous spirits and good heads on your shoulders. I am blessed to call each of you my own, and I respect and admire your good nature and your passion for living and learning. I love you.

Love and endless thanks to my sister, Michelle, thank you for EVERYTHING, and may you and your family be blessed with all the goodness in the world.

ACKNOWLEDGMENTS

To my agent, Ken Atchity, thank you for seeing my vision and devising ways to help me actualize it. I am grateful and appreciative of all you do on my behalf.

To Dee Gilbert, Stephanie Easton, Edie Hall, Phyllis Primus, and Rhonda Tatum, thank you for over twenty years of true friendship and support of my literary work. You ladies keep me grounded and keep it real!

To Linda King, my ace-boon-coon, who sells a whole lot of T.P.T. books for a Southern white chick! You are one of my very best friends in the world and I love you and your family dearly.

To Gloria Mallette, Mary Morrison, Karen E. Quinones Miller, Donna Hill, Alfreada Kelly, and all my literary sister-friends who are producing wonderful works of fiction while demonstrating a true spirit of sisterhood, goodwill, and friendship, may you each be blessed with the very best this literary world has to offer!

Finally . . . to my D.S.S. Crimson Tide line sisters in the most devastating, most captivating sorority in the world, Delta Sigma Theta Sorority, Inc. Ursula Sellars, Chandria White, Regina Williams, Anitra Albea, Denise Rogers, Altese Cabiness, Aisha Lubin, Marisa Moore, and Libra Forde. Through thick and thin, come what may, from the Deuce to the Tail, each of you have my love (and my white line shoes) forever! Oo-oo-oop! La Cosa Nostra! The Ace!

A NOTE FROM THE AUTHOR

I've been writing novels for sometime now, and I'm blessed to have produced works of literature that reflect my creativity, my diverse interests, and the wonderful gifts of my muse. While I don't always do things the way some feel I should, I am always true to myself, and that means that when I sit down to write a book I bring forth something fresh and new, distinct and colorful, each and every time.

That said, I simply cannot be accused of recycling previous stories or of giving my readers a new twist on an old rendition of any of my works. As different as *A Woman's Worth* is from *Knockin' Boots*, as sharp a contrast as you'll find in *Black Coffee* in comparison to *Gather Together in My Name*, you will surely find that *1-900-A-N-Y-T-I-M-E* is it's own unique work of fiction, a distinctive product of my muse that is unlike anything else I've written.

I'm sure there are those who would be more comfortable if I stuck to one genre and wrote the same types of books time after time, but there are also many others who are anxious to embark on new journeys with me, who are eager to explore new ideas and be tantalized by fresh and diverse stories! As a creative thinker and a lover of words, I receive great pleasure and immense joy in taking you, my reader, on an unchartered voyage where the only thing you can be certain of is a fantastic story and flawed, but compelling characters that you will grow to love, hate, and often understand.

As such, I invite you to open the pages of this book and experience life through the physical limitations of Bertha Sampson. Explore her desires and feel her pain. Allow yourself to imagine living life trapped in a body that cruelly inhibits you, yet is brimming with erotic passion and a soul that yearns to fly free.

And along the way, if you get lonely, or find you need someone to help fulfill your own special needs, well . . . you know the number. Simply dial 1-900-A-N-Y-T-I-M-E!

Peace and balance,

Tracy!

1-900-A-N-Y-T-I-M-E

SANG, BABY. SANG.

HERE she comes!" Bessie Morgan squealed over her shoulder, excitement ringing in her voice. "It's Little Bertha!"

Bessie held her breath along with the rest of Ebenezer Southern Baptist's congregation as a white-smocked usher pushed a wheelchair slowly down the center aisle between several uneven rows of rickety folding chairs. It was hot and crowded under the small revival tent, and some of the younger members had been forced to drag their chairs out onto the perimeter grass and expose themselves to the blazing Alabama sun.

Bessie sat with her knees pressed together in a make-shift second-row pew. She and her sixty-eight-year-old sister Nett had been organizing the church's annual visiting choir event for the past thirty years, and after an entire weekend spent in fellowship with nearly a hundred saints who had traveled from the surrounding bottom communities, her spirit and faith were nourished and restored.

Sweat trickled down Bessie's back and between her large breasts as she worked to stir up a breeze with a funeral parlor fan. For the past two days Ebenezer's congregation had been entertained by several organists and countless visiting preachers and singers, many of whom had garnered a small bit of fame for their foot-stomping, down-home gospel performances.

But according to the strange woman who had telephoned Bessie requesting wired money to bring her singer all the way from New York City, there was a singing saint making her way around the church circuit who could knock grown men to their knees and flood churchgoing eyes with righteous tears. The woman had insisted that her singer be scheduled to appear last on their program and had promised she would give them a gospel show that was worth paying and waiting for.

"I gotta pee," Bessie leaned over and whispered to her younger sister. The air was abuzz with anticipation and the congregation was unusually chatty. The influx of outsiders in these low country bottomlands was always a cause for excitement.

Nett frowned and angled her head. "What in the heck you reckon they got under that blanket?" She pointed toward the aisle, her eyes never leaving the strange entourage that had just made its way down to the pulpit. "What in God's world is *that?*"

Bessie craned her neck and stared at the wheelchair. A small form had been shrouded in the most beautiful hand-spun yellow blanket she'd ever seen. It looked like just a lump of something fleshy was underneath. Nothing was visible except a small pair of sock-covered feet, and in the blistering heat of the tent Bessie could have sworn those jokers were turned around backward.

Ignoring her bladder, Bessie watched closely as Pastor and Mother Williamson welcomed the group to the pulpit with broad smiles and open arms. Hank Brown took his fingers off the organ keys, and that high-yella Mabel Dinkins had the nerve to pirouette in her green whorehouse skirt as she handed the woman from New York a staticky microphone and grinned.

"Little Bertha thanks you," was all the handsome woman said before passing the microphone right back to Mabel. She stood behind the wheelchair calmly for a few moments, her eyes raking over the expectant congregation. She was cream colored with a mass of silver hair that had been hard pressed and hung around her shoulders. She had the air of a woman who had once been very beautiful and had grown accustomed to eager, appreciative eyes.

"Well," she finally said, "I s'pose y'all been waitin' long enough." She gave them a small smile, and then without another word she reached down and snatched the yellow blanket off the wheelchair and exposed a sight so horrific that all hell broke loose in the house of the Lord.

A woman screamed down front and Bessie Morgan started peeing right where she sat.

"God*damn!*" Pastor Williamson jumped back hollering, and Mother Williamson passed plum out.

"It's a demon!" Nett yelled, finger-pointing. "Them New York fools done dragged a goddamn demon up in here!"

Mabel Dinkins was on the move. Her fat arms flailed in the air in front of her as her thighs jiggled and her green skirt rose. She reached across Mother Williamson and grabbed a jug of holy water and started slinging it in every direction.

Hank Brown had never been what you would call a strong man, and it wasn't surprising when he leaned over his organ bench and threw up his dinner.

Chaos had come down on Ebenezer Baptist. A few bold boys ran outside to find sticks, while many of the younger children who had been sitting out on folding chairs were now crying and fleeing across the field, further down into the valley.

Bessie sat paralyzed as the woman from New York stood calmly behind the abomination, drenched in holy water as she held one hand high in the air. Folks were knocking over chairs as they rushed toward the back of the tent, and then the most incredible sound pierced the air, freezing every one of them in their tracks.

"A-a-a-*mazi*ng grace . . . how sweet the sound. Th-a-a-at *saved* a wretch like *meeee* . . ."

It was a siren so sweet, so pure, that Bessie, like the others, was stricken deep in the pit of her soul. Nett gasped and went stiff beside her, and Bessie wanted to fling herself to the ground and weep at the beauty that was falling from the mouth of what she could now clearly see was a very young girl, just past a toddler really, of no more than three or four.

"I once was *lost* but now I'm found. Was blind, but now I *seeeeee* . . ."

The child's head was huge and misshapen and positioned at the wrong angle on her narrow shoulders. Her right eye was missing and most of her facial skin looked raw and painful. She sang from a mouth whose upper jaw lay exposed in part, and her nose was a mere two slits that sat flat on her face.

Bessie was riveted, under a spell. The deformed little girl was like a pied piper. She spread her horrible lips and rang out with a voice that was holy and undeniable. She seduced them with her painful, enchanting song, and the congregation was held captive by her charms, forced to return to their seats as she baptized them in a spellbinding rendition of an old gospel tune that on this day had been reborn.

"Sang, baby!" Someone called out from the back of the tent. *"Sang!"*

Bessie could only stare. Little Bertha's twisted body had been clothed in all yellow. Her upper torso leaned left as her hips seemed to shift way right. Her feet were not turned backward as Bessie had first thought, but neither were they oriented for forward movement. Not that the child could have dragged her monstrous form anywhere without that wheelchair, Bessie knew. Her stumpy legs looked like they'd stopped developing early in the embryo stage and her neck seemed too frail to support the weight of her oversized head as it lolled toward her left shoulder, her chin touching her chest.

"That poor baby is *beautiful,*" Nett whispered, her

loving words coming in direct opposition to the disgust and repulsion that clearly showed on her face. Bessie turned to her sister and nodded. The entire congregation was similarly stricken. Their eyes may have been bulging with disgust and revulsion, but their hearts . . . their hearts and souls had surely been won.

CHAPTER 1

IT was 9:20 AM and Cho Lee Yung gripped the remote control and scowled as he stood behind the counter of Su Ming Yung Chinese Restaurant watching Sylena Scott on WNEW-TV. She was one of the ugliest black trolls in the mainstream media, and the only reason Cho tuned in to her show each day was to hurl new racial insults and criticisms her way.

Cho straightened up and smiled as the metal chimes tinkled and the front door swung open. His fourth customer of the day, a young black man wearing baggy jeans and a large platinum chain, swaggered in with a cell phone pressed to his ear.

"Yo, Chinaman, lemme get a large shrimp fried rice and two chicken wings."

Cho wiped his hands on his heavily soiled apron, bristling with anger inside. He was a small man, slight in stature but large in personality.

"Larr shreem-fry-riii?" he parroted with a big, accommodating grin. "Yes! Come riii up. You wan' drink?"

"Yeah. Lemme get one of them Sunkist orange joints. And make sure that shit is real cold too, man."

Damn niggers, Cho thought as he scribbled a few illegible numbers on a small white pad, then scratched a total at the bottom and circled it.

"Twell dollah fitty," Cho said, adding fifty cents to the correct total before pushing the receipt across the counter. He'd been working in Brooklyn a long time, and he always collected the money first. He watched the man pull out a thick roll of bills and peel off a twenty. Cho turned toward the cash register, hiding his grin. *Dumb fucks.* This was the third bill he'd padded today. It had become a big game with Cho. Each morning he'd wager himself on how much he could rack up in overcharges for the day, and by closing time the figure he'd calculated was hardly ever high enough.

Cho had a sharp eye. He could take one look at a customer and determine exactly how much he could stick him for. Sometimes he added a quarter to the total, sometimes it was a whole dollar or more. It all depended on how gutter and ignorant the customer looked.

Born in Bedford-Stuyvesant and educated at NYU, Cho spoke perfect English and had only left the United States twice in his entire life. His feigned broken English and Chinese accent were all a front, designed to give the impression that he was a dumb immigrant, fresh off a boat and still wet behind the ears. But in reality, Cho's family had come to America many years ago. And there was nothing Chinese about him, either. He was one-quarter Thai, and three-quarters Japanese.

Cho grinned. "You wan' duck sauce, yaa?"

"Yeah. Gimme some a' that soy sauce too."

Cho nodded, cursing himself. He should have added a whole dollar to this bill. The idiot had scooped up his change without bothering to count it. Drug money, Cho knew. Easy come, easy go. The people who walked through his doors seldom spent much time doing honest, honorable work. They spent their rent money on stylish clothes and expensive shoes, and they'd eat anything if it had enough salt and sugar in it. And that, Cho knew, is why storefronts and restaurants like his were so successful.

Cho reached behind his back and dug up his ass, then selected two of yesterday's chicken wings from the refrigerator and dropped them into a deep fryer of dark, coagulated grease. His dirty hands were a blur as he stir-fried week-old vegetables in a fiery wok. He'd learned how to cook this way from the elderly Chinese man who had sold him the restaurant many years earlier. The old man's instructions had been pretty simple: Exploit your customer. Maximize your profit on every grain of rice you sell. He'd shown Cho where to shop for scallions, peas, and broccoli that had been rejected by finer restaurants and were sold rotting by the bushel at cut-rate prices. He'd taught Cho how to rinse near-rancid chicken and beef in a mild solution of chlorine bleach in order to give them a longer shelf life. The successful Chinese restaurateur had schooled Cho in all the nuances required to ensure his complete capitalization off the narrow-minded ignorance of his customers, but the greatest pearl of wisdom he'd given Cho was the gift of patronizing his target market in a manner that made them feel powerful so that they would continue to come back.

Cho glanced over his shoulder at the young tough who was looking out the front window while barking orders into his cell phone. *Fucking idiot.* It was barely after 9:00 AM and fools like him were already pushing maximum

amounts of fat and sodium into their stomachs. Cho despised these people. Their ignorance and self-destructive
habits boggled his mind. Turning his back on the thug,
Cho bent over and parted his lips, then deposited a long
stream of saliva into the rice. *There. That should do it.*
Straightening up, Cho spooned the whole mixture into
a standard-sized take-out container and shook it around
a bit. Digging bare-handed into an open bowl on the
counter, he tossed six tiny shrimp on top of the fried rice
and carefully arranged them so that they appeared to be
plentiful and widespread throughout the dish.

Moments later the order was packed and ready to go.

"Larr shreem-fry-riii," Cho called out in his fake,
singsong Chinese accent. He waited until the man
turned around and could see him, then grinned and
piled packets of soy and duck sauce into the bag.

"I give you plenty soy sauce," Cho sang out. "Fortune
cookie for you too, 'kay?" He tossed three stale fortune
cookies in the bag as well, then neatly folded down the
edges.

The thug barely looked at him as he snatched his
order and cursed a long stream of displeasure into his
cell phone.

"Have nice day!" Cho called out at his back. "Come
back soon!"

The man stormed from the restaurant, throwing the door open so violently that it swung back and hit the safety stop that Cho had long ago installed, before triggering the overhead hydraulic switch that allowed the door to float to a peaceful close.

With a look of revulsion on his face, Cho waited until he heard the door's lock latch, then glanced up at the clock. It was 9:45 AM. He walked into his small cubicle in the back of the store, picked up his private line. He put it back down again. Too early.

Priming himself for the wait, Cho sank down on the worn cushions and unzipped his soiled work pants. Squirting a stream of baby oil into his palm, Cho looked around the shitty little office and sneered. "Damn niggers," he said again, and this time he said it out loud.

Cho Lee Yung had been born the third child in a family of five.

His father, Kido Yung, was a Japanese beggar whose family had toiled as laborers for generations in the ruling class's fields. His dear mother, Ming So Cho, had been born in Hiroshima and as a child had barely survived the United States' bombing of the city in 1945.

Rescued by strangers after wandering the streets

naked and bleeding, nearly all the skin had been burned from Ming So's face and from a large part of her body as well. The small child was not been expected to survive and had spent a tortuous year suffering from radiation poisoning and flitting between life and death in a poorly equipped hospice in a remote Japanese village.

Cho Lee had grown up hearing painful stories of his mother's early suffering and misery. He'd heard about how Ming So had come so close to death on one occasion that her radiation-ravished body had been shrouded and placed in a wooden burial box, and it was only the keen eye of an elderly Japanese woman who had saved her from being placed on the funeral pyre while still alive.

Ming So, though disfigured and scarred, had proved far luckier than most Japanese girls. She'd been adopted by the wife of a high-ranking American official and spirited out of Japan to the United States where she would receive the very best medical treatment from the countrymen of the same people who had nearly killed her.

Ming So's adoptive family grew very fond of her and she became stronger under their care. Five surgeries had restored a degree of elasticity to the skin on her face, arms, and back, yet the evidence of her trauma could never be erased and Ming So was seldom seen without some sort of shawl or blanket obscuring her face.

She grew up comfortable and provided for, afforded all the niceties that an American-raised girl of her status could expect. And although Ming So was sweet and kind and made friends easily, she had never fully recovered from her childhood trauma. Despite professional counseling, she was very self-conscious about the residual scarring on her face and as a young adult was often withdrawn and depressed.

Cho's father, Kido Yung, had met Ming So while working as a waiter at a dinner party given by her American family. Fresh off a smuggling boat and determined to build a fortune for himself in the land of opportunity, Kido Lee Yung had been stunned to find a Japanese girl living in such luxury with the Americans.

Accustomed to much hard luck and misfortune, Kido's heart had gone out to the girl. Not even the most destitute beggars in Japan suffered the way the survivors of Hiroshima and Nagasaki suffered, and feeling the pain of his countrywoman Kido reached out to Ming So, and on that night they fell in love.

Six months later, newly married to an American citizen, Kido Lee Yung moved his wife into the two-bedroom apartment that he shared with six other immigrant families in the Bedford-Stuyvesant neighborhood of Brooklyn, and with a small wedding stipend from

Tracy Price-Thompson

Ming So's American parents, they opened up their first fruit stand. Two years later, with two female infants in their arms, they purchased a small clothing store in a tough neighborhood, and following that there were three more babies—all robust sons—and three new grocery stores.

The Yungs were proud of their accomplishments. For immigrants from such meager beginnings they had done very well for themselves in their adopted American homeland. They shunned Americans and clung to all things Japanese. Cho Lee Yung, the oldest of the couple's three sons, had a quick mind for business and a soft heart for his mother. Plans were made and money was saved, and Cho was sent to New York University to study business and to prepare himself for the eventuality of running his family's businesses. One of his younger brothers was sent to medical school and the other off to Yale to study law.

Both of the Yung girls had inherited the artistry of their Japanese ancestors. The elder sister was heralded as a gifted flutist, but the younger sister was far more talented. She'd displayed the most amazing skill in ballet from a very early age and had studied dance at the High School of Music and Art. After a series of rave performances at Lincoln Center, where she was given numerous standing ovations, the girl was encouraged by an instructor to audition for Juilliard.

The family was ecstatic. Their ancestors had been laborers in Japan, and to have a daughter excel in the arts, a field long reserved for the ruling class, was simply astounding.

The preparation for her Juilliard audition was intense. Store hours were extended to generate extra income for private dance lessons, a sound engineer was hired to refine her musical accompaniment, and the entire family prayed for her success. On the day of the audition, Cho had been stocking shelves at one of the family's grocery stores when they got the call. Juilliard had the lowest acceptance rate of any institute of higher education in the United States, and of the many thousands of applicants who applied each year, only 7 percent were admitted.

Cho came out of the stockroom when he heard the excitement in his mother's voice. The look of pure joy on her burn-scarred face was enough to tell him everything, and the entire family was overjoyed. The girl had given the performance of her life. She'd danced so beautifully that her feet never seemed to touch the ground. She'd dazzled the panel of judges so thoroughly with her artistic skill and graceful movements that one female judge was compelled to approach her in the ladies' bathroom afterward and give her the unofficial news: her application to the Dance Division would be accepted by the performing arts conservatory, Juilliard School.

The entire Yung family rejoiced as they waited for the girl to make the hour-long trip home by subway. Kido Lee closed all three grocery stores early and invited their Japanese friends and neighbors over to eat and celebrate his daughter's achievement. Ming So and the older daughter prepared traditional Japanese dishes as they tried not to burst from glee.

But more than an hour later, the younger daughter had still not arrived. The family grew worried, and Kido Lee sent his three sons to the subway station to search for their sister.

Two hours passed, and then three. The neighbors left, the food grew cold, and Kido Lee and Ming So were deeply afraid. The girl had never been late before, and there was no reason she should be late now, especially on an evening when there was such a wonderful accomplishment to celebrate.

Three and a half hours after the girl's last call, there came another.

It was from a hospital in Manhattan, where the girl had been taken. The family rushed there by taxi-cab and the police spoke to Kido Lee, who was so weak he had to be supported by his sons. The police informed Kido that his daughter had been the victim of a random, violent crime. She had been severely beaten and robbed. Her assailants had stolen her wallet at knifepoint, then beat her badly and flung her down a flight of subway stairs when she refused to hand over the gym bag containing her dance shoes.

The fall, the doctors later informed them, had broken her neck. The fracture was in the cervical region and it was very severe. There was a high probability that the girl might never walk again, but it was still early, and the next forty-eight hours would bring a clearer diagnosis.

There was no describing the family's pain. Rage coursed through the girl's brothers, while her parents and elder sister could only weep.

"Who are these animals?" Cho Lee wanted to know. As the eldest male child he bore an obligation to defend his family. "What kind of men would do something like this to an innocent girl?"

"Men?" the policeman had raised an eyebrow. "These were no men." He passed Cho Lee a series of six mug shots that made his blood run cold.

They were girls. Young teenage girls. Young *black* teenage girls.

Even under the threat of severe criminal charges,

the entire group mean-mugged for the camera. Cho Lee could feel their ignorance and defiance radiating from the photos. Their sociopathic lack of remorse for crushing the hopes and ruining a young girl's dreams was evidenced by the anger in their dimwitted eyes and the insolent thrust of their jaws.

A tide of helpless bitterness rose in Cho that was all-consuming. Bedford-Stuyvesant was full of black girls like these. He'd looked down on them his entire life. Dressed like streetwalkers and flashing fake jewelry and outlandish hairstyles, they barged into his stores in large groups and stole whatever they could get away with. They always spoke too loud and their words were usually foul. They purchased items of clothing from his father's urban wear kiosk, wore them until they were visibly soiled, and then came back a few days later asking to exchange them for something new.

Cho saw no value in these people. They were self-debasing and did little to improve the quality of life for their own families. Their lifestyles and behaviors were so self-destructive that they permanently confined themselves to the lower rungs of society.

Years after his sister's beating, after his parents were both dead and most of the businesses had been sold, after his brothers had moved out of state and his eldest sister was married with children of her own, Cho Lee still grieved for his sister. Instead of dancing at Juilliard, she'd been paralyzed below the shoulders and confined to a wheelchair for ten years before succumbing to a deadly bout of pneumonia, leaving this cruel world with all her dreams deferred.

The journey through his past had left Cho cold. The disgust and contempt he harbored toward blacks was still palpable and had only grown stronger over the years.

He stared down at his pale member as it lay flaccidly in his hand, then looked at the clock.

It was time.

Damn niggers.

Forcing down his anger, Cho reached for his morning pleasure. He picked up the telephone and dialed a number that he knew would make him forget everything that ailed him, at least for the next fifteen minutes.

Holding the phone with one hand and himself with the other, he dialed 1-900-A-N-Y-T-I-M-E.

CHAPTER 2

A sultry ring tone jingled in the Purple Room as Bliss went about her morning routine. It was a hot, frantic beat over slow jungle drums, cut with soft sighs and moans of unmistakable sexual frenzy.

It was 9:52 AM and perched upon her double-wide crushed-velvet bench with cutout pieces of foam stuck between her brightly polished toes, Bliss ignored the phone and leaned closer to the vanity mirror as she applied a thin line of purple eyeliner to her lower lids. A smooth jazz hit drifted from the wall-mounted speakers and Bliss gently shook one swollen foot along with the rhythm, her mood just about set, her spirit peaceful and relaxed.

She'd spent the last hour prepping herself, and the bright purple thong and satin kimono she wore had been misted with fresh lavender. Two minutes later she'd gotten both eyes done and had delved into her makeup kit again when the melodic tune blared from her 1-900 line once more.

"All right!" Bliss muttered under her breath as she massaged café au lait cream blemish concealer into her soft cheeks. She batted her eyes in the mirror and grinned. "It's coming, baby. Don't be so damned impatient!"

Bliss prided herself on being a chameleon. A talented actress who provided top-notch customer service. One reason she was so successful at what she did was because she could talk about anything. Phone sex wasn't always about sex. People were usually looking to make a human connection, and on the phone Bliss came across as brilliant. Worldly and well-read. She'd practically raised and educated herself by watching television and studying over the Internet, and there wasn't much she hadn't explored.

She was naturally curious and every little thing in the universe was of interest to her. From the natural sciences to world religions, global politics, geography, ancient literature, astronomy, psychology, there was very little about the world that she didn't yearn to understand, and what she didn't know she simply researched from the confines of her apartment.

But a two-bedroom apartment had its limitations, and Bliss was human and she had her own human needs. In a way she got just as much from these calls as her clients did. And that was why, no matter how bad Bertha might be feeling out there in the Sick Room, it was important that everything about Bliss, from her hair down to her toes, be perfect each time she entered the Purple Room.

Depending on Bertha's health, Bliss's preparation time could fluctuate. On a good day she could be perfumed, oiled, and prepped for business in forty-five minutes flat. On not-so-good days she might have to toil over herself for two hours or more, but in the end it was all worth it and the cash that was transferred into her bank account each day was all the proof she needed.

Bliss had discovered a winning formula that kept her clients faithful and coming back for more. She accommodated them. She encouraged them. She indulged them. If they fantasized about a redhead, her hair was red. If they wanted a slut, she was the sluttiest bitch on the planet. If they wanted to know how wet her panties were, those suckers were *drenched*. Bliss was a professional, and she provided high-quality professional-grade service.

Which was one reason that she was comfortable with a ringing phone. She actually enjoyed letting the phone go unanswered because it was one area of her life where she wielded absolute control. Her clients called for *her*, she didn't call for them. She breathed life into their deepest fantasies. They needed *her*. She didn't need them. Besides, Bliss knew exactly who was on the other end of the line at this time of morning, and she also knew he'd continue to call every sixty seconds or so until she picked up.

"You ain't on my radar for another three minutes," she admonished the ringing phone with a soft giggle. The client's name flashed on her caller ID and Bliss checked her file and ran his credit card number through her system for a quick approval. There was no such thing as anonymity on a sex call. Bliss always knew exactly who she was talking to. The caller's billing information showed up as clear as day. Bliss nodded as his approval code came through. Yeah, old boy had great credit, but he was a control freak and a get-over artist. Always calling early and hoping to cop a couple of free minutes on the sly.

"Don't worry, big daddy," she cooed to the phone. "Just hold on and wait your turn. You're my first, sweetie, so you always get it fresh and hot."

Three minutes later the ambience was perfect and Bliss was ready for work. The lavender polish on her toenails had dried, and her long brown hair hung to her shoulders in soft, loose curls. Rising from her stool, she took a deep breath and gazed into the mirror, pleased by what she saw. Her lipstick looked hot, and already she was moist down below. A smoldering gaze had entered her eyes and a pair of delicate pearl earrings dangled sexily from her lobes.

Her round, custom-built party bed beckoned her. It was a huge lavender and purple throne with ten brilliant satin pillows and a thick, quilted satin covering. The sheets were made of expensive lavender silk, and Bliss sighed with pleasure as she slid her lower body between them and propped herself up against the firm pillows.

At exactly 10:00 AM the phone rang again, and this time Bliss was happy to answer it.

Cho had been dialing for nearly ten minutes and was overcome with need when the phone was finally answered.

"Hey, lover boy," the sultry, unmistakable voice of his fantasies caressed him through the telephone line.

"You've reached 1-900-A-N-Y-T-I-M-E, and you're in bed with Beautiful Bliss . . ."

"You've never done this before," Cho demanded. "Have you?"

"Never," she promised, sounding like a sexy college coed. "I'm nineteen and this is my first time."

"Nineteen and you're still a virgin?"

"I've been saving myself. For a sexy hunk like you."

Cho closed his eyes and sank further into the cushions. He'd reapplied the baby oil and his slick hand moved rhythmically in his lap.

"I won't hurt you," he promised. "I know it's your first time. I'll be gentle."

Soft murmurs fluttered into his ear. Bliss uttered innocent moans of pleasure as Cho began stroking himself into a frenzy.

"What are you wearing?"

"Purple," she breathed throatily. "I'm wearing all purple. A purple nightie and purple panties. Purple looks good against my pale skin, and it complements the color of my hair."

"Ummm . . . ?" Questioning.

"My hair is blond. You like that, don't you? It's silky and it smells like strawberries. It cascades over my shoulders and flows like spring water down my back."

The picture Bliss painted was perfect. Her voice, her speech pattern, her inflections were all those of a young, innocent—yet intellectual—college student. Bliss had been born with a vocal gift. Her voice never betrayed her. It implied neither black nor white, nor any other race or ethnicity. It was completely neutral.

"Are you pretty?"

"I'm beautiful. Breathtaking."

"Is your body like Angelina Jolie's?"

Bliss giggled like a perky cheerleader. "Even better. My tits are bigger and I have longer, sexier legs."

"Oooooh." Cho's voice was lust thick and Bliss made her move.

"Do you want to kiss me? Maybe on my thigh or my tummy?"

"No. Touch me," Cho demanded. "Put your hand on my chest and rub my nipples."

"Yes, what lovely nipples you have. As stiff as mine. Lie back," Bliss directed. "Let me make you feel good."

For the next twenty minutes Bliss rode Cho and he rode her too. He took her standing up, bent over a stack of crated potatoes, and on the front counter in his restaurant. He flipped her down onto the floor and pushed her legs over her shoulders, then climbed on top of her and rammed his penis into her while his head banged against a dusty stack of calendars that were left over from the Chinese New Year.

"O-o-o-h!" Cho stuttered as he squeezed himself three times then exploded in his own palm. His wheezing breath rushed through the phone lines as his toes curled with the aftershock of his beautiful morning orgasm.

Bliss waited patiently for a few moments, allowing him to catch his breath.

"Oh, Cho! You're so heavy." She giggled, still in character, still playing her role. "Sweaty too."

Cho sat with his eyes closed enjoying the last remnants of his fantasy. His fingers still worked over his flesh as he visualized the young blond-haired girl with the long, slender waist lying beneath him.

"Here," he said, rising from his knees in his fantasy and offering her his hand. "Allow me to help you stand."

Cho's expression changed drastically once the girl was on her feet and he saw the telltale signs of what she'd left behind on the floor.

"You are bleeding," he observed. He pretended to take a napkin from the counter and wipe at a rust-colored streak on the floor tile. He beamed with pride and pleasure. "You were honest. I *was* your first."

Bliss giggled in his ear.

"You were my first and my best. But I have a math class starting soon. College algebra. I have to go now, okay?"

"I'll see you on Wednesday, yes? I'll be your first again, right?"

"Of course," Bliss assured him. "I'll always be a virgin for you, Cho, baby. Every Monday, Wednesday, and Friday at 10:00 AM sharp."

CHAPTER 3

IT was nothing other than sudden death and a stroke of good luck that had landed Bertha in her present situation. The good luck came first, but the sudden death wasn't far behind it. Lurene Taylor, the old half-Indian woman who had raised her and pimped her across the country for almost ten years, had dropped dead from a massive brain stroke.

And *good goddamn bye* to her evil ass is what Bertha had thought as she sat in her wheelchair and looked down on the old woman's coffin as it lay in her open grave. Sure, Lurene had stepped up to raise Bertha when her own mother, a troubled thirteen-year-old relative, had abandoned her crippled, deformed newborn hours after giving birth, but altruism sure as hell wasn't in Lurene's heart when she did so.

"She wasn't nothing but a whore," Lurene often told Bertha of her young mother. "A funky-assed whore and a tramp. Slept with more mens than a banker could count. That's why you come out looking like you did. Got sperm cells from a hundred different daddies thrown together in you, gal. Ain't no way in hell you coulda come out lookin' right."

Bertha's uncle Long had told her a different story. He traveled the country with Lurene and Bertha, but he didn't have the same kind of cruelty in his heart.

"Your mama was a whore, Bertha. That much was true. But she knowed exactly who your daddy was. He was a military man. A good one too. He went over to Saudi Arabia and Kuwait and caught some kind of nasty chemical disease. They call it Gulf War syndrome and a lot of servicemen came back and had kids who was born looking just like you. Some look even worse."

What kind of whore her mother was or wasn't didn't mean a thing to young Bertha. It didn't matter how she got her birth defects. She had them. She saw the fear and disgust in people's eyes when they looked at her. The revulsion that made them clutch their hearts and run away from her as fast as they could. The only thing Bertha could do to erase that look was open her mouth and use her gift, which is why she sang so beautifully when Lurene took her to church on Sunday mornings.

"You could make a mint off the sound coming outta that ugly thing's mouth," the preacher at Lurene's small storefront church had prophesied. "Take her down south where they still revivaling in them backwoods and see what I mean."

Lurene had done just that. Hauling young, sick Bertha around the country on Greyhound buses and pocketing the cash that was eagerly passed around in sweat-brimmed hats had become Lurene's latest hustle, and young Bertha was little more than a cumbersome cash cow.

It didn't matter to the old lady that Bertha's afflictions were painful and embarrassing, or that they could be greatly improved by surgery and her physical appearance slightly enhanced. "The uglier the better," is what she said when a country doctor asked if she'd ever thought about taking the child to see an orthopedic or plastic surgeon. "That's the way God borned her and that's the way she's gonna die."

Indeed, Lurene enjoyed watching folks break for the nearest doors and windows when she snatched that yellow blanket off of Bertha. She'd stand stately and quiet amongst the chaos and hubbub as Bertha was screamed at, crosses were thrown, and holy water was flung at the small child by those who saw her as an abomination of the soul.

Lurene could actually feel her own power when she tapped Bertha on the shoulder and signaled the child to open her mouth and sing like a pied piper. The pure serenity of the child's voice, the spellbinding quality that entranced all who heard it, was so commanding and fascinating that despite her money-grubbing heart, Lurene herself often wept tears of joy.

Of course the tears didn't last long. Not much longer than did, say, the passing of the money-filled proverbial hat. Lurene and her small traveling entourage seldom stayed around for any length of time once they collected their cash. Even when Bertha was so sick and exhausted and road weary that she could barely lift her over-sized head, Lurene pressed her onward—hungry, diaper chafed, and propped up in a tiny bus seat, heading full steam toward their next gig.

This misery went on for several years, and young Bertha was powerless to change the state of her existence. That is, until one day when they stopped at a church in a town called Zinger, Mississippi, and Bertha met a man named Matthew Yarbridge.

Yarbridge was an entrepreneur in his late forties and a philanthropist for the physically disabled. His wife had died many years earlier, after giving birth to physically deformed twin girls. Yarbridge's daughters had been the apples of his eyes, but sadly, one twin had died shortly after her tenth birthday, and the other, while still alive, was far too disabled to enjoy much of a quality of life.

Bertha had just turned eleven that year and was growing extremely weary of being shaken and plucked like leaves on a money tree by the aging Lurene. They didn't travel quite as much as they once had, as Lurene was sick and getting up in years and Bertha had grown quite a bit and was no longer a toddler who was easy to tote around.

There had been a few times that rebellion had gotten the better of Bertha during one of their staged performances, and when given the customary cue and tapped on the shoulder by Lurene she had sat there mutely, refusing to open her mouth and entice their audience to return to their seats and open their wallets.

"*Sang*, goddamnit!" Lurene would pinch her shoulder painfully. "Heifer you better open your goddamn mouth and *sang!*"

Sometimes Bertha sang, and sometimes she didn't. On the days she refused and left Lurene standing behind her embarrassed and empty-handed, there was always a vicious beating waiting for her somewhere down the road. Lurene might have been getting older, but she was still money hungry and cock strong. She'd grab the old farmer's belt she carried around in her suitcase and reach back to Alabama and let it fly. Bertha would be at the old woman's mercy, writhing in her wheelchair, sometimes falling to the ground and flailing about in great pain and misery, but stubbornly refusing to use her voice for financial gain unless she absolutely wanted to.

Well, on this particular Sunday, Bertha wanted to.

Yarbridge was sitting in the front row with his daughter and her nurse when Lurene wheeled Bertha down the church aisle. The old yellow blanket had long been replaced by a bright yellow laced sheet, and Bertha's awkward-angled feet were propped up on the metal footrests.

Lurene went through her usual spiel. It was getting harder and harder to find small churches that were so deep in the woods that they hadn't yet heard of Bertha, and lately, Lurene had been forced to book gigs at a few churches that were in towns larger and a lot more worldly than she liked.

As usual, Lurene stood before the colorful congregation and waited until she had their full attention. Then she snatched the sheet off Bertha and got ready to watch the church house belch, shit, and empty itself out.

And the moment folks got a good look at Bertha, it just about did too. Everybody ran like hell for the exits except for the gentleman who sat up front with his own physically disabled daughter and her elderly nurse.

Lurene was suspicious as the well-dressed man sat gape mouthed and staring at Bertha with a strange look in his eyes. His three-piece suit looked tailored and there wasn't a speck of dust on his shoes. She took a good look at the grown woman who sat childlike beside him and quickly figured it out. With her funny-shaped head and a pair of legs that were almost as twisted as Bertha's were, it was no wonder this man didn't jump up and run. He'd seen his fair share of freaks before.

Bertha noticed the man watching her too. It was hard not to notice him and the two women beside him. They were practically the only church members left in the building. She opened her mouth and let fly her signature rendition of "Amazing Grace" and, as always, the beautiful siren's call reached outside the walls of the church house and pulled its members right back inside.

Several hats were passed around for Bertha that afternoon, and the largest donation of them all came from the man who sat holding his daughter's hand as he stared at her from the front pew.

"Good day." He startled Bertha when he walked right up to her and extended his hand. "My name is Matthew Yarbridge. Pleased to meet you. And what might your name be, young lady?"

This was a first, Bertha thought as she accepted the man's hand. In all her years of hustling church hats, never before had anyone approached her with anything that remotely resembled respect. Even after they got past the sight of her physical appearance, most folks took her for deaf and dumb. Adults would smile down at her and praise her singing in an artificially loud voice, but they reserved their greetings for Lurene, leaving Bertha propped up in her wheelchair to be stared at in revulsion and wonder.

Bertha soon got used to it. While Lurene milked the churchgoers with lies about finding Bertha on her doorstep on a dark and rainy night, Bertha would pull the yellow sheet back over her head until it was suppertime and Lurene wheeled her somewhere and pretended to feed her lovingly from a plate of country vittles that one of the church sisters had fixed.

But the man standing before her had walked right up and taken her hand. Ignoring Lurene, he'd addressed

Bertha directly, in a normal tone of voice, and was waiting expectantly for her answer.

"I'm Bertha," she said. "Bertha Sampson."

"And I'm Lurene Sampson," the old lady said, cutting between them. She nudged Bertha's chair aside with her knee. "I'm the girl's guardian."

Yarbridge looked down at the old woman and flashed her a bright grin.

"Guardian, you call it, huh? Well pleased to meet you too, ma'am."

He positioned himself closer to Bertha and directed his conversation toward her again.

"How old are you, Bertha? Where do you go to school?"

"She's nine," Lurene lied. "She goes to school way up north. In New York City."

Bertha saw a flash of excitement in Matthew Yarbridge's eyes.

"New York City, you say? Well that's a wonderful place for a girl like Bertha to be! Where at in New York City? What's the name of her school?"

Lurene moved behind Bertha's wheelchair and gripped the handles.

"Now why would I tell you all that, sir?" Her voice was highly indignant, but Bertha knew it was only because she'd been caught in a lie. "We don't know you! For all I know you could be planning something wicked on this here child! I tell you where she is all day and we might look up and find you waiting outside for her or something!"

Yarbridge laughed and held out both hands to reassure her.

"Oh! Forgive me! I didn't mean to alarm you–" He dug around in the jacket pocket of his expensive suit and came out with a card. "I'm Matthew Yarbridge of the Yarbridge Foundation for the Physically Disabled. It's a private nonprofit organization that helps disabled people who are in need."

He turned and pointed at the young lady who sat waiting for him on the front pew.

"That's my daughter, Cynthia. She was born with multiple physical deformities, but after a series of corrective surgeries she's living a very peaceful life, virtually free from extreme pain." The man leaned in closer to Lurene. "My foundation arranges the same type of care for others who can't arrange it for themselves. We especially like to assist the severely disabled and most times we can do it all for free."

"Uh-uh." Lurene turned up her nose and sucked her teeth scornfully. "I ain't letting none of them wacko doctors grab no knife and get to experimenting on my Bertha. Every time I turn around they killing somebody on the operating table, especially when you ain't paying them nothing."

"Well, have you ever taken Bertha to a surgeon to find out what was possible? When's the last time she's seen her primary care physician?"

"We don't *trust* doctors, mister. Besides, Bertha is plum scared of them. Wouldn't let one get near her if he tried. And surgery is out of the question. She's too afraid them folks might put her to sleep and kill her!"

He laughed. "I'm sure you're joking. Most surgeries are very safe these days! You can't let old fears stop you from exploring new things!"

"Who said we want to explore something new? Me and Bertha doing just fine working the old way."

Matthew Yarbridge leaned over and took one of Bertha's hands in his. His laughter was gone now and he shook his slightly graying head with contempt. He pressed something into Bertha's palm and spoke in a cold voice to Lurene.

"Old woman, save all that country-ass hogwash for the bootleg preacher who just ran out the door! This child might have been helped a long time ago."

Ignoring Lurene's cussing protests, he gazed directly

into Bertha's eyes. "Baby, you have what is called a cleft lip and palate. That's what's wrong with your mouth, you hear? It can be fixed. Easily. And I'm no dermatologist, but I do believe something can be done about your skin too. Who knows? With grafting and topical medication they might be able to make you more comfortable. Now, I won't pretend that I can stand here and diagnose everything that ails you, but both my daughters were born with spina bifida, and my gut tells me you might just have some form of that disease. In any case, there are lots of innovative treatments for spinal diseases these days, and"—he pointed toward Bertha's twisted feet—"whatever's going on with your legs could probably be evaluated by a bone specialist. All it would take is somebody giving enough of a damn to take you to the hospital so you can get the specialized care you should've been getting your entire life."

Lurene 'bout broke her neck getting Bertha and Uncle Long out of that church. They didn't even stay for supper, even though the church mother said the food was warm and ready to be served.

They caught a ride to the bus station, where Bertha sat grumpily in her wheelchair, hot and tired, watching dusty patches of country dirt swirl around her crooked feet. She was hungry and she had to use the bathroom.

"I need to pee," she declared and yanked Lurene's sleeve.

"Gone and piss in that diaper you settin' in."

"No, ma'am." Bertha shook her head. She hated going to the potty in a diaper like a baby. She would rather crawl to the toilet on her own, but Lurene said they'd get more pity and more money if folks had to imagine somebody wiping Bertha's big behind.

"See, they got a bathroom right over there." Bertha pointed to the bus station's restroom. "Unc can push me to the door and I can go by myself."

Lurene had turned and cut her evil old eyes so hard that Bertha was surprised they didn't pop right out of the old woman's head.

"I said piss in that goddamn diaper! It ain't gone kill you! You done did it plenty of times before!"

Bertha had no choice but to pee on herself, and she was still grumbling as the bus pulled up and Uncle Long carried her up the stairs and sat her by a window. She hated Lurene's wicked ass! And she hated the life she was living. She was tired of singing to strangers for pity money. Tired of riding Greyhound buses from coast to coast until her malformed back felt broken and her twisted legs went numb. She was tired of being dressed up in all yellow like a goddamn daffodil, and tired of pissing and shitting in diapers, then suffering the silent humiliation and shame of having the old woman cock her legs open, wrinkle her nose, and then wipe her ass like she was a baby.

As a growing adolescent Bertha was tired of a lot of things, but most of all she was tired of being used by Lurene. And perhaps that was why when, an hour or so later as she gazed out the window at the rolling countryside, all Bertha felt was annoyance as the old woman slumped over in the seat beside her, her head lolling heavily against Bertha's shoulder.

"Aunt Lurene," Bertha said, shrugging the woman off. She gasped in surprise when Lurene's body pitched forward and fell over in the seat, her yellow purse tumbling to the floor.

"Lurene!" Uncle Long hollered from the aisle seat across from his sister. He lunged for her and tried to sit her upright, but Lurene was dead to the world and promptly fell over again.

As concerned passengers left their seats to help, and the bus driver pulled over to the side of the road, Bertha sat quietly beside the woman who had raised her with a mixture of emotions rushing through her.

Things were about to change, she realized as she stared first at the motionless Lurene, whom folks had stretched out in the aisle and loosened her clothing as they tried to fan her back to life, and then down at the colorful business card that Matthew Yarbridge had pressed deeply into her hand. If what that man back at the church had said was even halfway true, there were doctors who might be able to help her get out of that dreadful wheelchair and start living a real life.

Freedom was too much to even think about as a flurry of activity surrounded her aunt, who hadn't moved a muscle since she'd keeled over on Bertha's shoulder. The possibilities stretched out in front of her like a long dirt road, and there was so much Bertha wanted to do, feel, and experience, that if she'd been capable, she would have gotten off that bus and wheeled herself straight down the highway! Sighing, Bertha dismissed all thoughts of her aunt, whose body was probably already going cold. In the midst of the chaos, Bertha closed her eyes and sat back in her seat and dreamed.

CHAPTER 4

BLISS sighed. Her first client of the day had been satisfied, and ignoring the pain that shot through her back, she wiped at a runaway purple streak under her left eye and took a sip of cool spring water. Romping with Cho could be very physical, and if he didn't insist on fucking a virgin first thing in the morning she would have preferred to take him on toward the end of the day when she had warmed up a bit.

She concentrated deeply as she washed off all traces of her previous look and tried to get her upcoming look just right. Her next client liked things soft and clean. No more of that bright purple and silver eye shadow or nasty pillow talk. Sweet whispers, pale lavender, and soothing shades of cream usually did it for him.

It was a chilly day and the dexterity in Bliss's hands was limited, forcing her to grip the makeup wand like a shovel as she steadied her arm against a tall bottle of Spanish cologne. Walkers and canes were strictly forbidden in the Purple Room, and Bliss's movements were pained but deliberate as she stood from her makeup stool and hobbled toward the short ramp several steps away.

Bliss surveyed the room with pleased eyes. It was a fantasy factory like none other. Everything in it had been paid for with money Bliss had earned from her own sexual creativity, and the furniture had been custom built to suit her particular needs and limitations.

Nearly thirty surgeries over the past fourteen years had been tough on young Bertha Sampson, but she'd survived each one by focusing on her determination to live her life to the fullest and to laugh and smile every day.

It had taken eight trips to the operating room to straighten her spine, five to rebuild her knees and properly align her feet, two intensive surgeries to place and then remove a drainage shunt in her head, one for her prosthetic eye, eight for skin grafting and the correction of her malformed jaw and cleft palate, and several other cosmetic procedures designed to make her look as normal as possible.

The results had been astonishing but certainly not miraculous. While Bertha was no longer the hellacious-looking child who traveled the church circuit scaring folks back to Jesus, she'd never stand tall or blend into a crowd, and venturing out in public could still be very humiliating and traumatic for her.

But thanks to Matthew Yarbridge and the Yarbridge Foundation for the Physically Disabled, a private foundation with an outreach component that supported independent adults with severe disabilities, Bertha required very little contact with the outside world. She lived in a rent-subsidized apartment provided by the foundation and received part-time nursing care from their paid staff. Her monthly living stipend was deposited directly into her online checking account, along with her small Social Security disability award, and she did her banking, shopping, and corresponding by Internet and telephone.

The only thing Bertha needed that the foundation did not provide was what she had provided for herself in the Purple Room, and with a cast of colorful and loyal clients, Bliss's sexual vices more than paid for themselves.

Scanning her surroundings, Bliss was pleased. Despite her various constant, nagging pains, she lived her life in high spirits by willfully rising above her physical limitations and enjoying the pleasures afforded by her salaciously sexy mind and the gift of her velvet-smooth voice.

There were many nights that Bertha tossed and turned in sweat-plastered nightclothes as she grimaced from the pain that radiated from her bones and ran haywire throughout her body. She'd refuse her nurse's offer of painkillers to numb her screaming joints and quell the wretched physical torment she'd known from the day she was born.

The medication, Bertha discovered, might tamp down the agony for a few hours, but it also dulled her senses, leaving her a foggy-headed fool for much of the next day. By the time she'd slept off her drug-induced haze, a beat would once more begin to rise in her bones, starting the cycle all over again and leaving her with large gaps in her memory and no recollection of the passing of time.

Bertha understood that many physically disabled people lived in such a state their entire lives. Consumed with pain, they were forced to ride their days out wrapped in a cocoon of protection from a body that was more like an enemy than a vessel of the soul.

But there had always been a big part of Bertha that

craved more. An aspect of her spirit that longed for a connection, an area of her body that ached for satisfaction.

Most people dismissed the thought of the disabled having sexual needs and desires, but they were dead wrong. Bertha had always masturbated. As a small child she had rubbed herself for comfort and to relieve boredom, and as she got older she did it for the same reasons everybody else did: it felt good.

But a late-night Internet session in an erotic chat room had really turned her out. A sexy conversation with a complete stranger had progressed into a hot bout of computer sex that had sent an orgasm coursing through her body that left her back sweating and her toes trembling. Just the power of the words, the visualization of what she and her nameless, faceless lover were doing to each other was so graphic and dynamic that it beat solitary masturbation coming and going. Bertha had slept good that night, no pain medication needed, and the next night she'd returned to the chat room for more of the same.

For a short while Bertha was content to get off on computer sex, but it quickly became impractical. With her disabilities it was difficult to type and touch herself at the same time, and more than once an impatient instant-messaging lover expressed his exasperation at having to wait for her to catch up in the conversation. Naturally innovative, it wasn't long before Bertha figured out that there was a much better way of working around her disabilities, and the second bedroom in her small apartment that had long sat unused became her sanctuary and her refuge. After spending countless hours researching, ordering, and communicating her wishes over the telephone and the computer, Bertha had a locked affixed to the bedroom door, a hard-core telephone line was applied for and installed, she'd recorded and then uploaded her advertising tracks, and she was ready. Her spare bedroom became a sacred purple place where pain and suffering simply did not exist, and Beautiful Bliss, the sultry, insatiable woman of every man's dreams, was born.

CHAPTER 5

IN most software circles Jim Burgess was considered brilliant. With a master's degree in computer engineering from MIT and a PhD in computer technology from Stanford University, Jim was sort of a demigod in programming, and he had more than his share of professional kudos and credentials to list on his résumé.

A softhearted fellow of tall stature and rugged, athletic good looks, Jim had been valedictorian of his high school class at Brooklyn Tech and had been offered full academic scholarships from the top five universities in the nation.

A city-bred boy who could sketch the Manhattan subway map from memory, Jim had chosen MIT because he loved wintertime in Massachusetts. He'd skied there with his father a few times as a teen and had fallen in love with the beauty of the state.

Jim's mother was a homemaker who had raised him with strict puritanical values. There was lots of prayer in the Burgess household, and in eighteen years of living under his father's roof Jim had never heard his parents raise their voices at one another or disagree strongly about anything in public.

Jim had been too consumed with his course work to go out on dates in high school, although there were several blossoming teenaged girls had caught his eye. He didn't consider himself a Jesus Freak, but he lived by a strong set of morals and values that guided his conduct, and on the night before his high school graduation, when a few rowdy friends from his senior class decided to sneak into the school gymnasium to drink beer and get laid, Jim had taken a few compulsory sips of Budweiser then hauled ass out of there as fast as he could.

With the taste of beer on his tongue, he'd ridden the subway all the way home to Bensonhurst fantasizing about what his friends were doing while he sat on the train with a gigantic erection in his pants. Julia French, the hottest girl in the senior class, had been one of the willing in that gymnasium, and she'd given Jim a look that told him it could have been his lucky night.

As it turned out, it *was* Jim's lucky night. Some old lady had heard a ruckus coming from the school gym and seen the lights on and had called the police thinking there might be a burglary in progress. The cops had burst in with guns drawn just to find themselves in the midst of a drunken teenage orgy.

Despite a slew of parental protests, everyone found on the premises had been charged with breaking and entering. The names of the offending students were skipped over during the reading at the graduation ceremony the next day, and the local newspaper ran a story with a snapshot of the school above a tagline that lambasted sexually promiscuous teens and the rising rates of underage drinking.

It had been a close call, and Jim had gotten down on his knees and thanked the Lord the moment he'd heard the news. It was only the hand of God that had led him out of that gym and back to Bensonhurst, because if Jim had obeyed his raging hormones and stuck around to try and get a piece of ass from Julia French, his would have been one of the names skipped over on graduation day.

Just the thought of getting caught up in a situation

like that was enough to sicken him. Not only would failing to graduate have jeopardized his academic scholarships, the shame and public humiliation forced upon his family might have killed them all. His mother would have surely taken to her bed in shame, and his father's eyes would have been filled with enough disappointment to burn down a rain forest.

After staying out of trouble and avoiding conflict during his entire four years of high school, Jim couldn't believe how close he had come to ruining his future, and he vowed to use the memory of his busted classmates as a life lesson to remind himself to consider all consequences and use good judgment at all times.

And for the most part Jim felt he'd done pretty well in living up to that vow. The variables that he could control about his life, he did, and those isolated incidents where he either fell victim to circumstance or was waylaid by malicious intent . . . well, in those cases Jim learned to look toward the Lord for his strength.

Jim stayed active during his college years and his clean lifestyle showed in his physique. He worked out each morning and ran at least ten miles a week. During the summers of his sophomore and senior years he had interned at Apple, and women took him to be much older than he actually was. They usually flipped when they found out that Jim was not only still an undergrad, but that he was also still single.

Single? they'd exclaim, studying his rugged, handsome face and well-toned, athletic body in disbelief. Not even a *girlfriend?* Well is he *gay?*

Those who knew Jim usually laughed. No, by all means Jim was not gay. Far from it. Jim was a Christian man who lived by the tenets of the Bible. And besides, he loved women. Almost as much as they seemed to love him. Jim was not promiscuous, but it wasn't because he harbored homosexual tendencies, although his father, mother, and grandfather would come to ask him that very same question several times over the next couple of years.

By the time Jim had earned his PhD and had yet to bring home even a casual date for his family to meet, his mother had started worrying too.

"You're our only son," she cried at Christmas dinner. "Will I get a chance to wrap gifts for my first grandchild before I die?"

Jim hated to disappoint his mother, but he hated lying to her too. The truth was, there would be no grandchildren in his parents' future. No daughter-in-law, either, as Jim was fairly certain that he'd never take a wife. He was working for Microsoft by now, dealing in some pretty heavy probabilities, and in his own life Jim knew the risks were way too high to be acceptable for such low rewards.

Sure, he had dreamed of getting married someday and he had always loved and wanted children. What blue-blooded American male didn't dream of reproducing and leaving his brilliant progeny behind? But because of *one night* of disgusting lust, Jim had been effectively robbed of all that, and the loss of a potential family was the sacrifice he was now required to live with.

The irony of it all was that as careful as Jim had been, as hard as he'd tried to use good judgment and make the proper decisions, it was someone else's hand that had loaded the magic bullet that delivered him a fatal gut shot. Jim had done nothing wrong on his own. Well, nothing that he had much memory of, anyway.

Everyone knows that college is often a time of great transition in a young man's life, and Jim had dreamed of attending MIT ever since he could remember. In his junior year, Jim and his close friend Chad Daley decided to pledge a fraternity together, and instead of his new brotherhood activities detracting from his studies, Jim quickly mastered the art of time management and balanced his life so expertly that he was able to be a well-rounded student and enjoy a decent social life at the same time.

It was the weekend before college graduation when everything fell apart, and although Jim wouldn't learn the true extent of the destruction that had been wreaked on him for another two years, the night in question, and the lingering aroma of his humiliation, would never again be far from Jim's mind.

On a warm night in late May, Jim and his fraternity brothers had bought quite a few rounds at the usual local haunts. Final examinations had just ended and every stringent requirement for graduation had finally been met.

"Whooo-hoooo! This shit is over!" Troy Gillette, a biology major, pounded Jim on the back and yelled into the late night air. There were seven members of Alpha Kappa Iota out celebrating, and the full moon shone directly overhead as they piled out of Troy's SUV and stumbled into the frat house.

They'd been bending elbows for hours and were already pretty well toasted, but that didn't stop Troy and a few others from rushing into the house to dig into their private stocks of gin, then stoking up a few loosely rolled joints to keep the party going.

"You buzzed?" Troy demanded as Jim flopped down on a worn sofa and grabbed a pillow.

"Yeah, man," Jim agreed, although he'd only had one beer. "I'm floating."

"Here." Troy snatched the pillow and pushed a lit joint into Jim's hand. "Take some pressure off! You're fuckin *graduating*, dude! Get a life! You look like you wanna crack open a fuckin' chemistry book, you asshole!"

Jim refused the marijuana, shaking his head.

"No thanks, man. I don't indulge. But you go right ahead. Don't let me stop you."

Jim watched as Troy swaggered off toward a rowdy group of guys who were flexing their muscles and shooting pool. Off along the far wall several other students were holding shot-tossing and dope-smoking contests, and still others were scheming on how they might get a few sorority girls to sneak into the frat house for a private party.

Jim sat there trying to look cool as he took everything in, and minutes later Troy was back in his face again, this time offering him a drink.

"Hey. Chad sent you an eight-ball. He said to tell you tonight is your night to get blasted *and* to get fucked!"

Jim just laughed. He was the only virgin in the fraternity, and several of his brothers had made it their personal mission to see to it that he got laid before leaving campus. It wasn't happening, but since they were back on campus and he didn't have to drive, Jim accepted the glass of liquor and sauntered toward the pool table eyeing his friend Chad with a grin.

Chad had been trying to hook him up with hot chicks for the past six months. It wasn't that Jim was some ultrareligious zealot who was waiting until he got married to get screwed, it was far less complex than that. Jim was simply waiting for the right person, that's all, and the moment she walked into his life he was absolutely sure that he'd recognize her.

And two years after that crazy-ass night in the frat house Jim was still waiting. He'd gone on to grad school at Stanford and after graduation nailed a great job with stock options and a solid benefits package with Microsoft. Jim began his new job on top of the world and was looking forward to scaling the steep corporate ladder when suddenly his foot missed a rung and his entire life came crashing to the ground.

"You'll have to come in to the office, Mr. Burgess," the nasal voice on the other end of the line had informed him. She was calling from the physician's office he'd been referred to by his new employer. Jim had selected the best benefit choices available from the employment package Microsoft offered, and a life insurance plan was part of their incentive. Jim had opted for a preferred whole life plan that had an annuity option, which required a physical examination before it could be implemented. He'd breezed through the exam a couple of weeks earlier, and now he was being told that there was some sort of irregularity in one of his laboratory results.

The nurse went on, "The law prohibits me from giving out any additional information over the telephone, however, I can schedule an appointment with our physician who will explain all of your test results in greater detail."

Jim had never been so surprised in his life. In fact, he'd actually laughed when the physician told him which of his labs had come back abnormal. It had to be a mistake. What the lab was reporting was impossible. He'd always been a straight arrow. A square, really. Jim didn't fit into any high-risk groups and he didn't have any self-destructive habits or practice any risky behaviors.

But there had been that one time . . .

Jim had shrugged the thought off.

Sure, it was totally fucked up, what had happened to him that night, but the odds of a one-time thing like that resulting in something as cruel and devastating as this were too long for even Jim to imagine.

But a month later the proof was staring him right in the face. The test had been retaken twice, the results processed at a different lab each time. And still they came back the same.

HIV positive.

Nothing could describe the myriad of emotions that Jim experienced over the next several months. Certainly fear and desperation had consumed him to no end, but the most pervasive and bone-shaking of them all had been shame.

One of the first things Jim had done was call his old friend Chad. It had been Chad who'd given him the narcotics-laced drink, and Chad who had snapped the photos that had been posted on the frat house bulletin board when Jim awakened naked and sticky on the rec room floor the next morning.

Chad had been full of apologies as Jim raged about the blurry details of that drunken, hooker-filled night two years earlier. Chad had sworn that it was Troy who'd laced Jim's drink with drugs, but it really didn't matter much who was responsible—the end result was still the same.

Jim Burgess was HIV positive.

Jim Burgess had a good chance of dying from AIDS.

The fact that Jim could barely remember fucking

the hooker didn't make the knowledge of the act any less painful. Certain small details from that night had managed to break into his consciousness and stay there. Like the way her fluffy brown ass had jiggled and bounced in his lap as she rode him from above. The unbelievable pleasure that had filled his groin and coursed through his entire body. He even remembered the scent of her perfume. It had been cheap and cloying, and just the memory of it made him feel light-headed and nauseous.

The photos Chad had snapped had been far from professional shots. There were only two or three where the whore's face was visible at all, and even those were blurry and partially obscured by her cheap wig.

But no matter how happy Jim looked in the photos, no matter how deliciously sore his balls had been or how tender the scuffed skin on his dick, no matter how eagerly his horny hands had cupped her breasts or how high his back had arched as he worked to thrust himself deeper into her, Jim *knew* he had protested. He could recall brief images of his fraternity brothers roaring with laughter, urging him and the girl on. He'd tried to fight and he was sure his heart had been unwilling, but the proof was in the pictures and his body had been highly cooperative.

Much more than Jim Burgess's virginity had been stolen that night. He'd been robbed of his future as well. His friends had shelled out cash for a hooker, and she'd given Jim their money's worth.

Plus a whole lot more.

And now, after a lifetime of balanced choices and living according to his principles, the well-intentioned actions of a few drunken frat boys had wiped out all of Jim's efforts in a single fuck.

There was simply no way to share that kind of news with his parents. It would kill his father and grandfather on the spot, and Jim's poor mother would probably go into a coma or suffer a slow, agonizing death. So instead of sharing the weight, Jim weathered his burden all alone. He accepted his fate with the same practicality that he'd lived his life. He worked out religiously, ate properly, learned what he could about natural herbs and remedies, saw his doctors regularly, and allowed his family to believe he was a bit of an eccentric . . . or secretly gay.

Over the next few years a cloak of loneliness blanketed Jim's world that simply couldn't be penetrated. He'd dropped his request for premium life insurance and had been hired on at Microsoft with a standard benefits package, and sure, on the outside he was still the same brilliant, outgoing, good-natured all-American guy who was invited to every barbeque, cocktail party, and social event in town, but on the inside there was always a battle raging. A battle between his shame and his disease, and no matter how he looked at it there seemed to be no conceding on either side.

There was no more football, basketball, or soccer for Jim. He gave up contact sports, afraid of the remote risk of being injured and exposing someone else to his tainted blood.

And as for women, Jim forced himself to go without. Sure, he was a normal man and for certain he had his needs. Jim loved women, worshipped them, actually, and put them on lofty pedestals to behold. He socialized pretty heavily: dinner, movies, a couple of low-pressure social dates. His sexual energy was high, but the thought of unwittingly exposing, and thereby victimizing, someone else was out of the question.

No, Jim was a good, honest man, and there was no way in hell he could jeopardize anyone else's life the way his had been so carelessly jeopardized. He would never be able to live with himself if he practiced such trickery, for he had a pure heart and a gentle spirit, and only two vices to speak of, one of which was his enduring hatred for filthy blacks, and the other that had actually led him to a wonderfully pure white woman who satisfied his needs on nearly every level.

He imagined her to be tall, healthy, and athletic, with soft blond hair and a beautiful but virtuous smile. He knew her to be warm, chaste, funny, and smart. Jim found the girl of his dreams very easy to talk to. She was friendly without being too flirty, and so well educated that she seemed to know a little bit about everything under the sun.

If ever there was girl who Jim felt in his heart was the right one for him, this girl was it. Their chemistry was perfect and they were explosive together, and Jim could tell by the sadness that sometimes crept into her voice that she carried her share of secret pain too, just the same as he did. They talked on the phone for hours, about all sorts of things, and he never tired of hearing her smooth, beguiling voice as it liltingly caressed his ear. It was costing Jim a small fortune to maintain their relationship, but no more than it would have cost him to take her out on dates or to buy her the kind of gifts and jewelry she deserved.

It was a crazy twist of fate that the telephone had brought them together, but there was also an element of safety in that kind of distance too, Jim knew. The last thing he would ever want to do was expose her to the terrible burden that he carried. He cared about her far too much to do that. The only thing Jim wanted to do was love her, to give her the limited parts of himself that he was able to share, and with these warm thoughts on his mind and a cavernous yearning for a connection in his heart, Jim picked up the telephone and dialed 1-900-A-N-Y-T-I-M-E.

Bliss?" His voice was soft, tentative.

"Yes, Jim," she answered pleasantly. "I'm here."

This was her most gentle call of the day, and he always put her in a good mood.

"How's it going?" he asked. "Did you sleep well last night?"

Bliss giggled. "I sure did," she assured him. "I stretched a bit longer before taking my jog, like you suggested, and when I was done I came home and did a few of those back exercises you emailed me, then took a cool bath. I slept like a newborn."

"How were your meals? Remember," he teased, "what you eat is what you look like!"

Bliss laughed. "Oh, I ate extremely well yesterday," she lied. "Five small meals. Mostly proteins and veggies. It was great."

Tracy Price-Thompson

"Did you drink any extra water?"

"I did! Two extra bottles, and I took my calcium and iron supplements as well. Thanks to you, Jim, I'm healthier and feeling better than ever."

"Good! I'm glad some of my suggestions have helped."

Bliss covered her legs with the soft sheets and closed her eyes, settling deeper into the fantasy. According to the client, he was an ultrabusy and successful software engineer from a wealthy Republican family with Southern roots. Bliss viewed her calls with Jim less like sex and more like a form of executive stress relief. From their frequent conversations Bliss had learned that he was a health enthusiast, the outdoor type who worked out regularly, ate right, took lots of herbal supplements, and drank tons of water. He was also mild mannered and a little nerdy, but Bliss actually liked him.

"Your suggestions are always helpful. And that's why I want to help you too, Jim. Right now I'm lying here on my sofa wearing the kind of dress that you love. It's long and white, made of sheer cotton. It's very modest, of course, you know that's the kind of girl I am, but even still . . . it's hard to hide my athletic curves, you know what I mean?"

His voice was heavy. "I know."

"My hair is pulled back," Bliss whispered in her soft, enthralling voice. "I washed it this morning and it still smells of fresh summer melons. You like that scent, don't you?"

"Oh, I do. Yes."

"Sit beside me, please? It's a bit chilly in here."

"Sure," Jim said, playing along. "Your skin is cool. Your arms are so firm and toned. You take good care of yourself, Bliss. I really like that."

Bliss led Jim through some of his favorite foreplay moves. She pulled up her shirt and urged him to lay his penis in the valley between her firm, round breasts.

"Ahhh, yes." She sighed. "Slide it back and forth," she whispered as Jim's breathing deepened and soft gasps escaped his lips. "I've poured baby oil over my breasts, Jim. Do you like that? Can you smell it? Is it warm enough for you? Yes . . . keep stroking me just like that. My breasts are so large and soft. My nipples ache terribly. Would you like to rub them too? Ah! They're slippery and stiff! Yes, that feels so good!"

By now Jim would be pretty worked up. He'd usually want to flip her over onto her stomach so he could cover her bottom with tender wet kisses, then he'd ask if it was okay to spoon for just a bit. He liked to lay with his nose next to Bliss's neck while she described the sweet scent of her own hair.

"Let's snuggle for a while, okay? I know you have to leave soon, and I can't stay long, either."

Bliss would grin and glance at the clock on the far wall. It wouldn't take Jim long. It never did. For some reason he never wanted to penetrate her. He was usually satisfied just by kissing her, touching her, and hearing her voice. It was puzzling to Bliss, but Jim made sure she knew he was wearing a condom at all times.

"I'm so hard right now," he'd say. "Watch as I put on my condom, dear. I would never touch you without one. I care about you, Bliss. I'm protecting you."

One time they were going at it hard and strong. Jim was rubbing his dick around in her soft blond pubic hair and he slipped the head inside of her by accident.

"Goddamnit!" he'd yelled. "Oh, my God. I'm so sorry, Bliss. I entered you! It was a mistake, dear. I promise you, it will never, *never* happen again."

Bliss didn't know what the big deal was, but Jim had been apologetic for weeks. He'd emailed her all kinds of "please forgive me" cards and insisted he'd never meant to sully her.

Whatever, Bliss had thought. Her job was to play along with the fantasy, so she had cut up like a teenager whose boyfriend had stolen a half ounce of pussy.

"Oh my goodness! You put it in me! Slid it right in! It was hard, Jim! Hard and thick!"

Jim had made it up to her by giving her some wonderful phone head. He was ultragraphic in his description of all the ways he could eat her pussy.

"I won't take off your panties," he moaned. "I'm only pulling them to the side, okay? This is safe, Bliss. I've checked it out. It's no different from kissing, so it's safe."

Bliss repaid him by performing for him orally too. Only she wasn't allowed to say any dirty words and she wasn't actually allowed to put his naked penis in her mouth.

"Just kiss the condom, dear," he instructed. "Don't open your mouth too wide. Just small kisses will do."

Bliss really liked Jim. He was weird as hell, but she had no problems indulging his fantasies. After all, it was a fantasy that the man was paying for, and Bliss was always happy to deliver.

CHAPTER 6

MIDDAY was always a relaxing time for Bliss.

In addition to their great conversations, phone sex with Jim usually brought her to at least two orgasms, and if his oral sex in the flesh came anywhere near close to the way he described it over the telephone, his real-life girlfriend was one very lucky chick.

Bliss had heard Jim say over and over again that he was single and wasn't in a relationship, but she no more believed that bullshit than he should have believed she was five nine and a hundred and twenty pounds of sweet-smelling white flesh. The fantasy was great, but Bliss was always careful to keep it all in perspective, even when her clients couldn't. They were paying her for a service that she delivered damned well, and as long as their credit card charges were approved prior to the call, they could tell her anything under the sun and she'd giggle, nod, and agree.

Hunger was settling in the pit of her stomach and Bertha's home attendant would be arriving soon. Bliss stretched her short limbs, then climbed carefully from the bed. Her mind wandered as she peeled off her soaked panties and balled them up in the towel she'd used to wipe the sweat from her body.

Back at her makeup table she used cold cream wipes to clean her face, then pulled her hair back in a pony-tail. She put away her purple panties, scarf, and bra, then stepped out of the virginal white linen dress she'd worn briefly for Jim and hung it back in the closet.

Transitioning from one room of her apartment, from one dimension of herself to the next, required a lot of work, but Bertha was up for it. She controlled these small elements of her day and demanded the ordering of her two selves. She made it a rule never to wear sick clothing into Bliss's Purple Room, or allow any erotic clothing into her Sick Room. That kind of transfer of energy simply wasn't allowed. Instead, Bertha transitioned between rooms wrapped in a large bath towel, keeping her two personas completely distinct and independent.

Besides, she had to keep all traces of Bliss hidden from Hyacinth, the home health aide who had been with her for nearly ten years and was more like a mother than an employee. Hyacinth had never seen the Purple Room. The door was kept locked at all times and the only key hung around Bertha's neck.

Locking the door to the Purple Room, Bertha shuffled behind her walker into the handicap-accessible bathroom, where she held on to the stall rail and took a quick shower. Hyacinth was a professional neat freak, and towels, shower gel, prescription skin ointments, and other toiletries were laid out neatly, and within reach.

Washing away the scent of Bliss's perspiration, Bertha ran down her afternoon schedule in her mind. Mornings were a breeze because as long as she was feeling okay the night nurse usually left by 6 AM. The bulk of Bliss's phone work was done between ten and two, when Hyacinth's shift began, although she could usually sneak away for a few minutes in the evenings or at night if a client needed her to.

The rest of her schedule for today would be pretty light. She had a few short calls scheduled, none of them her major clients, just a couple of quick hand jobs that she could probably fit in when Hyacinth stepped out to do some shopping or laundry. Sneaking her calls in while someone else was in the apartment was a challenge that Bertha welcomed. It broke the monotony in her life and added a thrill to her day.

She had just toweled off and was rubbing skin-strengthening ointment on her face when she heard the wind chimes tinkle on her front door.

"Bertha?" Hyacinth James called out in her comforting Southern voice. She could hear the fifty-seven-year-old woman moving around in the kitchen.

"I'm back here," Bertha answered, cracking the door. "In the bathroom."

Bertha slipped into a simple housedress and, sliding her walker out in front of her, headed toward the kitchen.

"Hello," the older woman said, then hugged Bertha briefly and kissed her cheek. "How's my pretty girl feeling today?"

Bertha just smiled. Hyacinth was a longtime employee of the Yarbridge Foundation and she'd been assigned to her care shortly after Lurene's death. Hyacinth was an excellent nurse and an even better friend. She had six children of her own and five ex-husbands, and it was pure luck that Bertha had met her. Her aunt Lurene's body wasn't even stiff yet when she'd pulled out the business card that Matthew Yarbridge had given her at the church and dialed his number.

Matthew had come for her immediately. He'd brought her back to New York and set her up as a ward under his foundation's care, and he had been helping her become an independent adult ever since.

One of the first things Matthew had done was arrange to have Bertha examined by a team of specialists, and after it was determined what kind of help was available for her, he arranged for her first surgery. Hyacinth had been one of the nurses who attended to Bertha during her long period of recuperation, and they'd taken to each other. More than ten years later they were still together, and Hyacinth had become part mother, part conscience, and part sister to Bertha all at once.

"I'm hungry," Bertha said, lowering herself into a chair. Hyacinth hated to cook and Bertha had never learned how, so the pair usually ordered out for lunch each day. There were so many delivery boys coming and going to Bertha's apartment that the lobby manager downstairs had long since stopped detaining anyone who came bearing a package of hot food for delivery to her apartment.

"Well, it's Monday." Hyacinth shrugged. "I guess that means we're eating that horrible Chinese food you love.

How you can tolerate that type of poison in your stomach I don't know, girl."

Bertha laughed. The old woman loved the sweet and salty Chinese dishes just as much as she did. "You say that every Monday, Hy, but yet and still, you eat it."

Hyacinth shrugged. "What else am I going to do? They pay me to take care of you, you know. You think I'm going to let you eat that poison alone? No, I'll call."

Hyacinth dug into a bin stuffed with menus below the wall-mounted phone.

"It's Su Ming Yung's," Bertha told her. She could recite the telephone numbers of at least twenty different restaurants from memory. "The number is 555-7812."

Hyacinth ordered shrimp fried rice and sweet-and-sour chicken for herself, then placed a special order for Bertha's unique one-of-a-kind dish that had become so familiar to the Chinese man on the other end of the line that Hyacinth could barely get the beginning of the order out of her mouth before he was completing her sentence.

"Yep, you got it. Same as always. All of that mess doesn't even sound right mixed together. I've been trying to get the girl to order something different, something that makes sense, but she's hardheaded, I tell you."

Thirty minutes later Bertha and Hyacinth sat in the living room eating Chinese food and watching the Tyra Banks show. A panel of guests were discussing the light-skinned/dark-skinned challenges that plague black people, and Elizabeth Atkins, a biracial woman from Detroit, was explaining to the audience how skin color biases can damage relationships between people of color.

"Hmph." Hyacinth shrugged. "This country has always had some blacks this color and some that. Everybody knows the white man treats the lighter blacks better."

Bertha couldn't relate. As her alter ego Bliss, she dealt with people of all races and ethnicities, and while she was smart enough to know how horribly race and skin color affected the world, she spent so much time living in other people's fantasies instead of interacting with real people that she hadn't really experienced it much. Besides, the skin pustules she'd been born with had left her pretty neutral on the color chart. Even after all the grafting and medications, her skin tone was neither darker nor lighter than a paper bag. It wasn't brown or black. It was such a scarred mosaic of tissue that it was just Bertha.

"There's trouble at the foundation, you know,"

Hyacinth said as she finished the last of her lunch. Bertha noted that despite her earlier protests, her caregiver had eaten every bite on her plate. "Not enough money."

Bertha looked up. The foundation had been the bedrock of her existence for over ten years. All of her surgeries, her financial support, her private nursing care . . . The foundation did so much good for people like her that she couldn't imagine it going under.

"Mr. Yarbridge sure doesn't look broke. Besides, I thought they had benefactors. Rich people who made big donations. Dead people who bequeathed their entire estates and whatnot."

"It's not enough," Hyacinth answered. "I heard donations have fallen off. The economy is bad. Plus medical costs are rising sky-high. The more people Mr. Yarbridge helps, the more people that are left who still need help."

Bertha felt a chill in the pit of her stomach. She calculated her small disability allowance plus what Bliss made from private calls in the Purple Room. With her rent, multiple prescriptions, and private nursing costs, if she lost the foundation's support she couldn't begin to pay her bills.

"So what are they going to do? Shut everything down?"

Hyacinth gave her an incredulous look. "Close it down? Does Matthew Yarbridge look like the shut-it-down type to you? The man is a genius. He'll figure something out. Right now they're going to do a big telethon to raise a lot of quick money. You know those? The kind where organizations broadcast their requests for donations on television and people call in their pledges all night?"

Bertha had heard of telethons before. She'd watched a couple that were held to benefit AIDS sufferers, and what American hadn't seen Jerry Lewis's yearly telethons that supported the Muscular Dystrophy Association?

"That's a good idea. Maybe he can get a bunch of actors and celebrities to cohost with him."

Hyacinth nodded. "Matthew will do even better than that. He's going to bring some of his recipients and beneficiaries on to help. He's rallying young people just like you who benefit from the foundation's grants and programs. This is a wonderful chance for you guys to give something back. This is how you can repay that generous hand that's been feeding you all these years."

"Nah, I couldn't do it." Bertha shook her head quickly. "It's a great idea and all that, but I'm not getting on national television begging nobody for money."

Hyacinth looked surprised. "And why not? Are you too good to ask for help?"

Bertha shrugged. She wasn't too good. She was too shamed.

"You're one of the foundations biggest success stories, Bertha! Matthew is counting on people like you. You accept the man's help every day but you're too ashamed to give some back?"

"I'm not saying that." All those years of being wheeled to the front of a church just so folks could scream and run and throw holy shit at her came flooding back. Bertha had done her time as a freak on display. Let somebody else pass around a goddamn hat. She was done with all that.

"I'm just not getting on television, that's all."

"Bertha." Hyacinth sighed. "That's one of our biggest problems! We have a large population of physically disabled people who are too ashamed of being seen in public! How do you think you can touch people's hearts if you hide yourself away from them? Sure, you have your physical limitations, but who among us is perfect in this world? The more people see, the more they know. The more they know, the more they feel. What do you think your life would be like if there had been no fund-raisers before you came along to the foundation?"

Bertha shrugged.

"There would have been no money!" Hyacinth

exclaimed. "Child, look at what was done for you! You've had countless surgeries! Schooling! Somebody like me had to nurse you 'round the clock! Who you think paid for all that? It didn't come cheap! Those things took a lot of somebody else's money, you know!"

Bertha shrugged again. She had real love for Matthew Yarbridge. Real love. While Bliss entertained the fantasies of strange men in the Purple Room, Bertha built her own fantasies around Matthew in the Sick Room. She wanted him the way a real woman wanted a real man. In the flesh and in the spirit. That man had given her more in the last ten years than anybody had given her in her entire life. Every day when she got out of bed, she knew it was Matthew who had made it possible for her feet to touch the floor. When she put food in her mouth she knew it was because of a man like Matthew that her palate had been closed and she could swallow without choking. When Bertha looked in the mirror and saw a body that was once twisted so bad it made folks cuss and piss their clothes, but had become much less hideous under the skill and care of surgeons who donated their time because of their allegiance to the Yarbridge Foundation—she knew it was Matthew Yarbridge who had made it all possible.

It wasn't that she didn't want to help. She did. Bertha

was grateful for the life she was living and there wasn't a damn thing she wouldn't do for Matthew, and in whatever room he wanted it done in. She'd been dreaming about him since she was eleven years old, and if her knight in shining armor had so much as hinted like he wanted her to be his princess, Bertha would have rushed up in that big black castle he lived in and rocked his world inside out. No, she couldn't think of too many ideas she wouldn't jump on if Matthew Yarbridge merely snapped his fingers. She just wasn't getting on national TV.

"Remember, Bertha," Hyacinth warned, "somebody steps up and puts themselves out front for you every day. The foundation is bigger than your fears, baby, so get past them. Matthew needs you, and the foundation needs you too."

Bertha picked over the last bit of beef with lobster and peanut sauce on her plate and looked at the clock on the microwave. It was time to shut all that telethon nonsense down. Hyacinth always went grocery shopping after lunch on Mondays and Bertha needed her to get going so that she could shuffle her ass back inside the Purple Room where Bliss would set out a warm jar of baby oil and her favorite dildo, then get ready for her afternoon hand game of "stroke and choke the chicken."

CHAPTER 7

LATTRELL "La-Rule" Johnson leaped up on the stage to a multitude of flashing lights and a round of thundering applause. He waved to the adoring crowd and gave them his biggest, sexiest grin. In Lattrell's world there was a hell of a lot to smile about. He was in the prime of his life and at the top of his game. His killer-grill was plastered on the cover of every hip-hop magazine from New York to Los Angeles, and in addition to having the most lucrative recording contract of any rapper in the game, he'd recently been tapped to star in a movie depicting hard life and crime on the streets of Atlanta.

Lattrell had it all. His luck was great and his pockets

were full. With sold-out high-capacity concerts and four #1 hits in a row, his last two albums had dominated the Top Ten charts and he had more groupies and devoted fans than he knew what to do with.

Success hadn't come overnight for Lattrell, but it hadn't taken him half as long as it took some artists to get on. In addition to the hard-core street message that he rapped about in his music, there was something about his long, chiseled body, inner-city swagger, and bomb cornrows that had captivated the young urban set, and despite the decline in CD sales that most artists were suffering from, Lattrell's stock just continued to climb as radio stations and urban nightclubs blasted his music over and over again each day.

He was on cloud nine as he grabbed the microphone and began chanting his latest blockbuster hit with all the gritty emotion and edge he could muster. "Yeah, motha-fuckers, the name is LATTRELL! I'm a bad-ass rapper, two T's, two L's!"

Everything about Lattrell was camera perfect. Standing six-feet-five, his bulging muscles flexed, his skin shining with stage sweat, he rocked impeccable braids and sported diamond earrings and a foot-long platinum rope chain.

He had his boys with him on stage too, backing him

up on vocals and handling the overflow of gorgeous honeys that were screaming and crying out and desperately
trying to climb on the stage just to get a touch of him.

"I wanna suck your dick, Lattrell!" a female who was
pressed against the edge of the stage screamed out as
she held a large sign bearing the same message over her
head. "Suck the 'ick' outta Lattrell's dick!"

Lattrell just laughed and did his thing. He was easy.
He was in his element and doing everything right. Doing
everything that was expected of him. He performed four
songs straight, two that featured Phe-Nom, a competing
artist who was on the rise, and when his boy came on
stage to join him the two of them took the crowd to an
even higher level.

They were in a rapping frenzy as the music pumped
and they recited their verses, strutting all over the stage
with their chests poked out, giving the crowd everything
they expected and more. They pulled two sexy chicks
up on the stage with them and slapped their asses, then
bent them over and simulated deep stroking them from
the back.

An hour and a half later Lattrell's voice was hoarse
and his clothes were soaking wet as he exited the stage
to a standing ovation. Security flanked him on the left
and the right as his boys fell back and let him have his

space. Lattrell headed toward his dressing room, paus-
ing to sign a few autographs before going inside and
locking the door. His ears were ringing from the ultral-
oud music and his heart still beat wildly in his chest as
he dropped the grin he wore in public and peeled off his
wet shirt.

Lattrell had a strict set of after-performance rituals
and it had taken him a minute to get his entourage to
understand and respect that. They all wanted to pile up
in his dressing room and smoke blunts and bask in the
glow after a performance, but that was the time when
Lattrell craved his solitude the most.

He stood before the mirror, checking himself out.
He was a rugged, good-looking guy with light brown
skin and a killer's glare that had taken him months of
practice to perfect. He glanced at his sculpted pecs and
washboard abs as he toweled himself dry, and he could
see why women stayed on his jock and fainted with pleasure at just a hint of his smile.

He was a groupie magnet, and all the thrown thongs
and flashed titties could wear a brother out. But still, Lattrell kept a slew of the most beautiful women available
around him at all times. He viewed them as necessary
accessories, like fresh sneakers or multi-jeweled grillz.
Groupies were image enhancers, and boning them and

tossing them off is what a man like him was expected to do.

Lattrell grabbed a beer from the minibar and lit his ritual after-concert blunt. Eyes closed, he went over his entire performance in his mind, confirming to himself that every movement, every word, had come out right. The proof had been in the crowd. You couldn't afford to take a misstep in this game. Fans would turn on you faster than shit, and where you were king one day, you could be suspect the next.

Lattrell had done his time at the bottom of the heap and he'd vowed he'd never get down that low again. Born outside of Athens, Georgia, Lattrell had been one of ten children in a family that lived and breathed religion seven days a week. Washed and oiled, the Johnson clan spent every evening in the small converted farmhouse that Lattrell's father ministered from. Reverend Jasper Johnson was an ex–heavyweight prize fighter who worked two low-paying manual labor jobs to support his large family and then preached from the farmhouse well into the night. His mother was a good-hearted seamstress who sewed for a wealthy woman in town.

The fourth son of six big, rowdy boys, Lattrell and his brothers were known for their superior height, physical strength, and athleticism. They played football and

basketball and ran track, and the older boys took up boxing and power lifting. But even though Lattrell was great
in the ring, the spitting image of his brothers, and was
just as big and strong as all the Johnson boys, it was obvious to everybody in the family that he was different.

"Lattrell is in the girls' room!" his younger brother
Duncan yelled to his mother one Friday afternoon, bust-
ing Lattrell out for the second time that day. "He's braiding doll hair again!"

Lattrell had knocked his little brother down getting
back to the narrow bedroom where all the boys slept.
He loved brushing and combing the huge doll heads
that his sisters always got for Christmas, and he could
out-jump all three of them in double-dutch and was a
better hip shaker and hand clapper too.

Lattrell's brothers got a kick out of spying on him
and then dropping a dime to their father, who lived by
the Word and shunned effeminate behavior in males
as an abomination before God. Lattrell could hear his
brothers laughing and calling him names from the other
room, and his eyes were cast downward in shame as his
mother came in from the kitchen drying her overworked
hands on a dishcloth.

"La-La," she said, calling him by the pet name she'd
given him and putting her slender arm around his broad

shoulder as she sat him down beside her on a bed. "You know your daddy don't like it when you disobey him, don't you?"

Lattrell put his head down and tried to burrow his big self closer in his mother's arms.

"Now Daddy done already told you to stay outta the girls' room, honey. He said no doll babies, no jump rope, and no braiding hair, okay?"

Lattrell had frowned, then nodded. There was love and sadness in his mother's soft eyes, and he only liked it when she smiled.

"Son, you just gotta stop all that," his mother insisted. "You can't be having all them girlish ways and I mean it. The last time Daddy boxed you he liked to kill you. I love you, Lattrell. You Mama's La-La baby, and I don't want him beating on you like that no more. Okay?"

"Yes, ma'am," Lattrell said.

"Good," she said, standing up and giving her son a bright smile before heading back to the kitchen. "Why don't you sit and read your Bible for a little while? If you learn all your verses maybe Daddy'll let you sing at service tonight."

If there was one thing Lattrell loved more than creating jazzy braid styles and swiveling his hips, it was singing. Contrary to his sweet, girly ways, by the age of twelve Lattrell's voice had matched his large, muscular frame, and when he threw his head back and belted out hymns in church he brought forth such a powerful sound that even his father beamed and smiled at him with pride.

It was after one such performance at church that Lattrell's life changed forever. He was fifteen years old and his oldest brother Javon was getting married to a sweet girl named Lordina from their congregation. There was a hub of activity buzzing around the church, and the aunts, cousins, and sisters of the bride and the groom were busy hanging up decorations and bringing in food for the reception.

Lattrell was just under his full height of six-feet-five, and walking through the throngs of wedding guests in his white three-piece suit and rented white patent leather shoes, Lattrell knew he looked good.

Reverend Johnson was officiating at his son's ceremony and there was a reception scheduled immediately following the wedding service. Lattrell couldn't wait to get the show started because he was the guest singer and would be serenading his new sister-in-law on behalf of his brother.

Things couldn't have been going any better. The wedding ritual was joyous and upbeat, and Lordina's large, happy-go-lucky family blended well with the big, overgrown Johnson clan. Lattrell was the center of attention as he sang Lordina a love ballad dedicated from his brother, and something came over him as the crowd rose to their feet and enveloped him in thunderous applause. He stood there grinning, his smile spreading from one wall to the other as the wedding guests gave him a standing ovation that blew his mind and almost lifted him into the air.

Lattrell's head was still in the clouds ten minutes later as he walked out of the reception hall and headed toward the men's room. He shook hands with guests in the hall and hugged friends and family who were milling about as they congratulated him on his performance and made him feel like a big star.

Lattrell had used the restroom and was washing his hands at the sink when one of Lordina's cousins came out of a stall. Reggie Flanders was a tall, skinny guy with light skin and soft hair. He wasn't a regular at the Johnson church and only made a couple of obligatory appearances with his mother around Christmas and Easter. He was a few years older than Lattrell, about eighteen or nineteen, and even though they'd never run in the same circles, Reggie had always been friendly whenever their paths crossed.

"Hey man!" Reggie said, joining him at the sink. "I didn't know you had pipes like that! You really blew it up in there. Good job."

Lattrell blushed. "Thanks. Yeah, you know. I sing a little bit."

Reggie laughed and tore off a paper towel. He grinned at Lattrell in the mirror. "I wouldn't call that no little bit. You got a throat on you, boy. A real deep throat. Check this out. I know this club right up the road a bit near Atlanta. They play a little jazz some-times. They always looking for good singers. Maybe we can hang out sometimes and I'll show you where it's at."

The older boy held Lattrell's gaze in the mirror, and there was something about the way he smiled that made Lattrell blush again. Harder.

"That sounds cool, man," he answered as Reggie dried his hands. "Sure, one day we can hang out."

"Yeah," Reggie drawled. His voice was low and thick. He let his gaze travel down Lattrell's broad chest and then linger on his crotch.

"I like your pants," he said.

Lattrell felt a knot jump bold in his drawers. His let his gaze imitate the older boy's as he stared at Reggie's crotch in return. Lattrell sighed and bit his bottom lip.

Reggie's dick was so long and hard the print showed halfway down his thigh. "I like yours too."

Reggie laughed, then nodded. He held the door open and let Lattrell walk out first. "Yeah, man. You and me gonna get . . . together. One day."

Lattrell strode out of the bathroom with his dick hard and his fists clenched in his pockets. He had only taken five or six steps down the hall when he felt a large hand sweep across the seat of his pants and grab a big handful of his ass.

Lattrell jumped and behind him, Reggie laughed.

"You missed!" Lattrell yelped, whirling around to face the young man with a big grin.

But the grin froze on his face when Lattrell realized that Reggie wasn't the only person walking behind him. Reverend Johnson had come out of the bathroom too. He'd been using the toilet in a stall, and to the horror of his son, the good reverend had seen and heard everything that had gone down.

Hell had no fury like a reverend shamed.

"Papa, no . . ." Lattrell raised his arm instinctively to protect his face as Reverend Johnson barreled toward him with his fist drawn back. But it wasn't Lattrell the preacher was aiming for. It was the gay man who recognized the homophobic fury in the pastor's eyes but didn't have a chance to duck before he was felled like an ax-struck tree.

Reverend Johnson was a big, strong man. Even bigger and stronger than any of his sons. When his oversized fist tore through Reggie's face it busted his nose, knocked out his two front teeth, and fractured the young man's lower jaw.

With bright blood dripping from his hand, Reverend Johnson turned slowly to his left, never coming out of his boxer's crouch. Ring-rage burned in his eyes, and when they lit upon his son, poor Lattrell threw his head back and screamed like a bitch because he knew exactly who was getting clocked next.

"Papa! I didn't—" the words were snatched from Lattrell's mouth as his father slammed his palm against his chest and gripped his suit jacket in an enraged fist.

Reverend Johnson lifted his six-foot-plus son off his feet with one hand and flung him toward the bathroom with enough force to crack Lattrell's head against the doorframe and send another scream tearing from his throat.

"Papa!" Lattrell writhed and yelped from the floor. "I swear to God, I didn't do nothing!"

Reverend Johnson advanced on his son. His voice was a low, cold growl.

"You lying, unnatural, unholy . . . filthy . . ."

"Papa!" Javon called from the end of the hall. He'd been dancing with his new bride when a rush of panicked guest had pulled him off the dance floor to come see about his father. "What you doing, Papa? What's going on?"

The entire wedding party had pushed out into the hall, along with nearly all the guests. All eyes were on the scene playing out in front of the men's room and the only sounds to be heard were the shrieking cries coming out of Lattrell's mouth.

There was some initial confusion in Javon's voice, but after moving closer and taking a look at the gay man who was knocked out on the floor, and then another at his weeping younger brother who lay terrified under their father's glare, it wasn't hard to figure the rest out.

"Dammit!" Javon shook his head in anger. The eyes of almost everyone he knew in the world were boring into his back, and humiliation broke him out in a cold sweat. He glared at his younger brother in disgust. "You little *faggot!*"

"Nooo," Lattrell heard their mother wail from the crowd. "Don't say that!!"

Javon met the cold look in his father's eyes with one

that was just as frigid. He turned and scanned the crowd of people who had come out to celebrate the most special occasion of his life and scowled. The mood of his day had been soured. Lattrell had ruined it for them all. Searching for his brothers, he found similar looks of disgust in their eyes as well.

Javon turned back to his father.

"What are we gonna do, Papa?"

Reverend Johnson looked down at Lattrell, then back up to his eldest son who, like his other four boys, was sturdy and reliable and without a doubt all man.

"Get the congregation ready, son. We're gonna pray."

Nothing could have hurt Lattrell worse.

Or humiliated him more, either.

"Strip," his father had told him after pushing him back inside the men's room. The wedding guests had been ushered back into the reception hall. His mother had wanted to come to him, and Lattrell could hear her crying and being comforted by one of his sisters as they forced her to go back inside the hall.

"Sir?" he'd asked.

"Strip," his father repeated. "I ain't beating my clothes."

Lattrell had taken off his beautiful white suit with shaking hands. He'd stopped at his underwear and looked up at his father, whose eyes indicated that he should take those off too.

Standing naked in the men's room, Lattrell had prayed for God's mercy and understanding. His eyes were closed and his lips were moving in supplication when he felt the first blow.

It caught him flush on the temple and almost knocked him out.

"I'm going to make a man out of you yet," his father vowed. Posturing like the ring champion he had once been, Reverend Johnson hunched his shoulders and balanced himself on the balls of his feet.

The next blow was a gut punch and it drove Lattrell backward and slammed him up against the cold wall. Bile rose in his throat and a trickle of urine dribbled from his penis as he grabbed at the wall and tried to stay on his feet.

"Papa . . ." he whispered.

"Papa, *hell*," his father whispered. "Call on your Holy Father up in heaven, son. Ask him to wipe clean those wicked, unnatural ways that are going to get you killed up in here today unless you denounce that demon who has taken hold of your soul, son."

"I denounce it!" Lattrell screamed, eyeing those killer fists that were balled up and aimed his way once again. "I denounce it! I denounce it! I denounce it!"

"No," his father said calmly. He advanced upon his son with the same brutal tenacity he'd used when stalking an opponent in the ring. "You don't denounce it yet, my child. But you will."

Fifteen minutes later there was blood on the men's room walls. The floors were slick with it and the stark white suit that Lattrell had taken off and laid across a sink was splattered red like a painter's smock.

The wedding guests were huddled at their tables in the reception hall, murmuring in hushed tones. The music had been turned off and Javon and his brothers were standing near the head table waiting anxiously for word from their father. They'd heard the screams coming from the men's room and understood that their father was doing what needed to be done.

Their mother sat with her eyes closed between two of her daughters who were wiping her tears and fanning her damp face. Every few moments her body would jerk and she'd moan out loud, as though she was being physically struck, and her daughters would whisper their comfort and hold her down in her seat.

A sound was heard and all eyes were on the door as

an usher opened it and Reverend Johnson stepped inside. He stood there drenched, unsteady on his feet, the naked body of his son lying limply in his outstretched arms.

There rose a collective gasp and Mrs. Johnson cried out as her husband entered the room cradling their bloody son and walked slowly down the center aisle. The reverend's shoes clicked on the hardwood floor as Lattrell's head lolled back on his neck, his buttocks sagging in his father's embrace, his arms hanging loosely by his father's legs.

"Oh, dear God, Jasper!" Mrs. Johnson screamed. "Did you kill him? Is he dead?"

Laying the naked body of their son on the floor, Reverend Johnson turned to face his wife and his entire congregation.

"No, Jewel. I didn't kill him. Lattrell is not dead. But the demon that was living inside of him sure is."

Reverend Johnson signaled his other children, who rose from their seats and came to the center of the room and stood near their quietly weeping brother. One by one they placed a hand on Lattrell's bloody body and uttered a prayer of protection for his soul. And when they were done, the entire congregation stood and followed suit. They formed a line that snaked twice around the room and waited their turn to lay a healing hand on Lattrell Johnson and beseech God to slay the young man's unnatural demon and heal his twisted, broken soul.

The last person on line was Reverend Johnson.

The reverend's body was tired, his muscles spent and sore. He had fought longer battles in his life, but none as difficult or as worthy. He gazed down into the swollen, tear-streaked face of the begotten son he so deeply loved and asked God for both forgiveness and strength. Not for himself, but for Lattrell. It was a tempting world out there and this was only round one. There would be other battles for Lattrell to fight. Other demons. Reverend Johnson could only pray that Lattrell would be strong enough and fit enough to go the distance.

And if nothing else, strong Lattrell was. His father had beaten more than spiritual muscle into him that long-ago day. And after tonight's performance Lattrell felt good. Up on that stage, exposed under the public's eye, he had done everything right. He'd behaved exactly the way the world expected him to behave, without a demon to be found anywhere in his act.

Gangster certified and packing a tool! I'm the hard-core street nigga known as La-Rule! The hype magnet! The ladies screamed Lattrell! Get it right all you haters two T's and two L's!

Toking his blunt and inhaling the weed deeply, Lattrell allowed himself to relax on the soft black sofa. He was coming down off his stage high slowly, just the way he liked to, but he knew it would take more than the blunt to put him totally at ease.

What Lattrell needed was some ass. He slipped his hand down the front of his pants and fondled his already thickening rod. Stroking off was an option, but it would only piss him off and make him want what he wanted even more. Sighing, Lattrell held on to the log in his pants and retrieved his cell phone from the edge of the end table.

With incredibly demonic thoughts crowding his mind, Lattrell dropped his well-rehearsed façade and dialed a number that both exhilarated him and shamed him at the same time. With visions of a skinny light-skin boy and his father's swinging fists in his mind, he dialed 1-900-A-N-Y-T-I-M-E.

"It's time to party and you're banging it up with Bliss . . ."

"Yo, sexy. What it looking like, baby?"

In the Purple Room, Bliss yawned. La-Rule was the only client she allowed to call her in the middle of the night. Because of his occupation he kept weird hours, and even though Bertha wasn't really crazy about getting up to play "head" games with him after his shows, he only called once a week or so and he always sent her freebies and promotional items that made getting out of her warm bed and dragging herself into the Purple Room worth her trouble.

"Ain't nothing happening over here. I'm about to chill with my man, Neck. He's on his way over to my crib so we can get busy."

"Oh yeah? What kind of night you and Neck got planned?"

"I don't know yet," Bliss answered, playing along with the game. "We might get something to eat and maybe smoke some sticky. We'll probably fuck most of the night, though, because for a skinny yella fella Neck sure got a nice long dick."

"Damn." Lattrell laughed. "That's your man and you be putting his business out on the street like that?"

"Oh, he don't care," Bliss said. "Neck is proud of his package. He don't care if the whole world knows what kind of weight he's carrying. If he could walk around with his dick hanging out without getting arrested, he would."

More laughter. "So it's like that, huh? That nigga Neck must be special. I've never met a man like that. I don't think I could be that bold, even if I had a real big dick."

"It ain't just his dick," Bliss said quickly. "It's his balls too. Neck has the fattest, fluffiest balls you've ever seen. They feel like little furry peaches in your hands."

"Peaches?"

"Yep, peaches. They're soft and fuzzy, but thick and bouncy too. And you should see the way they smell. Oh my goodness. There's something about Neck's balls when they get sweaty. They give off this scent that drives me crazy. I mean, there's nothing like it. I stick my nose between them and sniff so hard the little hairs start tickling me!"

"Oh, that's some funny shit!" Lattrell said. "I bet ball hair on your nose makes you wanna sneeze, huh?"

"No, actually it makes me want to lick. And suck. Oh my goodness, Lattrell. Neck's dick gets so hard when I sniff his balls! To be so skinny that dude's dick is almost like another leg! I like to slide the tip of my tongue right along the line on his nut sack . . . yummy. Doesn't that sound delicious?"

"Ummm . . . I bet you like it, huh?"

"I do. I hold on to that dick with one hand and lick

those big sweaty balls until they're bouncing all over the place!"

"Yeah . . . what Neck be doing, baby? Do he give up the ass too?"

"Neck loves giving up the ass. He pulls his cheeks open and lets me lick that ass out so good! He goes crazy when I toss that salad, and sometimes he likes to stroke his own dick while I'm tonguing his rim."

In his dressing room, Lattrell was now naked on his back with his long muscular legs gaped open.

"Oh . . . shit . . . tell me how he strokes it . . ."

"Neck squeezes the head, then pushes the skin back as he fists it to the bottom. He keeps up a nice rhythm too."

"Do you suck them balls for him? Do Neck like it when you suck them balls?"

"That's almost the best part. Neck likes to feel dick up against his balls, though. He likes it when I strap one on and rub my dick all over his balls, then press the tip of it into his ass."

The unmistakable sound of a meat beating was coming through the phone line, and although Bliss was happy to be servicing her client, this was one fantasy that gave her no personal pleasure.

"Do you ever put your dick in him? Do Neck like to get fucked in his ass?"

"Yeah, he do, but my strap-on don't do him right. Sometimes Neck gets mad because I don't have the thing he really needs."

"Oh yeah? Too bad. Did I just hear your doorbell ring? Neck is probably out there trying to get in right now."

"Well let his ass wait! I'm busy talking to you!"

"Nah, baby. Crazy as that nigga is? The way he be tossin' dudes around? Don't get your ass kicked over me, baby girl. Go head and let ya nigga in. I'll wait."

"You sure? I mean, I don't wanna just cut out on you like that or nothing. You was here first."

"I'm sure. That fool is a straight-up thug. He's got a criminal rep. But if you scared of him just let me know, sweetheart."

"I am scared. Real scared. Would you stay here with me until Neck leaves?"

"Me and you cool like that. I'll stay as long as you need me to. I just hope I don't have to bust nothing in that nigga's ass over fuckin' with you."

"Would you do that for me? I mean, I would feel so much safer if you stayed. I really need you to be here."

"Aiight, baby. You ain't gotta beg. Go let that big-dick nigga in. I'ma chill right here in your closet just in case he gets stupid on you. Just don't let him know where I am, okay."

"I won't," she said. "Your secret is safe with me."

"You promise?"

"I promise."

"Cool. Hurry up. Don't keep Neck waiting no longer. Let him in."

Bliss pretended to open a door, then she whispered, "Hey, Lattrell! Can you see us?"

"I see you, baby. Go 'head, doll. Handle your business. Don't worry about me. Attend to your man."

"Damn," Bliss reported, "Neck's dick is hard already."

"Mine too."

"Ahhh, I've got my tongue in his navel. I love the way he smells."

"Go on, girl. Suck his dick. I'm right here with you. That nigga got them big-ass balls bouncing all in our face!"

"Do you smell them?"

"Oh, hell yeah! I smell 'em. I taste 'em. I feel them fat, nasty things all over my lips."

"Help me," Bliss pleaded. "Neck got too much dick for one person to handle. Help me out with some of this."

"Girl, you know I got your back. Let me get a little bit of that for you. Ahh, yeah. This nigga tastes just as good as you said he did. Dick all fat and juicy. Hitting the back of my throat. I wanna taste that cum too. I can help you out there, if you need me to. Damn! Where'd this guy get these big, pretty-ass balls?"

"Rub your dick on them," Bliss directed. "Neck likes to feel dick on his balls."

"Make him . . ." Lattrell's voice was thick and he could barely talk any more. "Please. Tell Neck to . . ."

"Oh my goodness!" Bliss shrieked on cue. "Neck! What you doing!? Why'd you ram your big dick up this man's ass? Stop it, Neck! You *stop* it! Lattrell is not GAY! Oh my goodness. He's holding you down, Lattrell. This big nigga done flipped you over on your stomach and he is fucking the hell out of you! That horse dick is pounding all in your ass and he won't stop! I can't pull him off you! He's too strong for me. He's going deeper and deeper and I can't make him stop fuckin' you!"

Lattrell screamed into the phone line. It was a sound so torturous with pleasure and pain that Bliss had to hold the phone away from her ear.

"Fuck me, Reggie!" the young rapper cried hoarsely as he exploded with the orgasm of his dreams. "Bust this ass open! Ram that big dick up in me, baby!"

Bliss glanced at the clock. Lattrell had done well tonight. Sometimes it took a little time to coax him out of the closet on these calls, but once he was out he sure had a lot of fun. The young man on the other end of her line was still screaming out directions to Reggie, his imaginary lover, as Bliss went about straightening the Purple Room so she could be ready for her morning clients the next day.

Lattrell was going to have an early morning too, but he wouldn't be getting a wink of sleep tonight. Because unbeknownst to Lattrell, his boy Phe-Nom, the second-ranked rapper on the U.S. charts and Lattrell's chief money rival, was standing right outside of his dressing room door. He had come by with love, just to tell Lattrell that a limo was waiting for him outside, but then ended up hanging around to listen in amazement as the number-one ranked rapper on the U.S. charts took a dick up the ass from some unknown dude named Reggie.

CHAPTER 8

FELICIA Browning had always been a beautiful woman, and her current circumstances didn't render her any less so. At fifty-eight, her smooth cinnamon skin still held traces of youth, and her lush brown hair, always the focus of someone's attention, still shone with strength and fine texture as it cascaded around her pillow.

"What are we having for breakfast?" she asked her husband of thirty years as he reclined at her bedside, caressing the soft skin of her hand.

Gary bolted upright in his chair. The sound of her voice was startling. It had been such a long time since he'd heard it, and like most things about his wife other than her physical appearance, it had drastically changed.

Felicia was a patient at the Family Hospice of New York, a New Age long-term-care facility and a division of Sloan-Kettering Cancer Center. Gary had chosen to bring her to New York for Family's respite care because its policies were geared toward providing a comfortable and relaxing atmosphere for terminally ill patients during their final days. Family Hospice was the best in the country. It catered to the needs of the patient and provided beds, meals, and other amenities for spouses who chose to maintain physical closeness with their mates during their illness.

Gary had dressed Felicia in her favorite fall colors: rust, muted yellow, and burnt orange. Her mosaic-patterned jacket was made of an elegant grade of silk, and her dress was a solid shade of brown. The beautician who'd been styling her signature mane for the past twenty-five years came by once a week to visit her friend and to keep her "do" tight, and one of the younger staff members was nice enough to lightly apply Felicia's make-up each morning when she came on shift.

Gary Browning patted his wife's hand and spoke to her in a normal tone of voice.

"Soon, baby. We'll grab a little something to eat soon."

He gazed at the small table near the window where

the remnants of the meal he had fed his wife no more than ten minutes earlier still lay.

"I have a panel meeting at seven," Felicia reminded him in her strange, coarse voice. "The grant proposal is just about complete, you know. All we're waiting for is the final review."

Gary smiled and nodded his understanding, unable to speak.

Felicia had been one of the top biochemistry scientists in the country, and prior to taking sick she'd been working on a major research project through the National Institutes of Health. The Institute had brought in another researcher to head the final phase of the project, and the grant had been completed and approved nine months ago.

Gary watched his wife as she gazed briefly toward the wall, then settled back on her pillows and closed her beautiful eyes. Soon, her lips grew slack and slight snoring noises escaped her mouth as Felicia found a measure of peace in her morning slumber.

Before today Felicia hadn't spoken a word in more than five months, and her doctors had warned Gary that her loss of speech, memory, and clarity were all a part of her disease progression. The type of tumor she had grew deep inside her brain and it continued to challenge the medical community because it was inoperable and thus rapidly fatal.

The Brownings had been married for more than three decades, and while the past few months had been extremely difficult for Gary, he was loath to complain. He would have loved to spend the next thirty years with the girl of his dreams wrapped in his arms each night, and certainly he would have climbed into that hospital bed and traded places with Felicia in an instant if he could have, but Gary was a scientist and a realist. Bad things happened to good people all the time, and neither he nor Felicia was exempt from the misfortunes that were sure to arise simply from living one's life.

Besides, they'd had more joy and adventure during their marriage than most couples even hoped for. While Felicia was a native Chicagoan, Gary was a country boy from Mano, South Carolina, who had been determined to get a top-notch education, explore the world, and leave the universe a better place than it was when he found it.

An only child, Gary's mother had died of a blood clot shortly after his birth.

"One minute she was right here, loving on the both of us," his father would recount years later, still shaking his head in grief and disbelief, "and the next minute she was gone."

Gary learned later that things hadn't happened quite that quickly, although he was sure it seemed that way to his dad at the time. His mother had actually suffered from a blood clot in the leg that broke off and lodged in her lungs. She'd gone into a coma and lingered on life support for several days before being declared brain-dead, and according to his aunts who had helped raise him, his broken-hearted father hadn't let go of her hand once the entire time.

Life could get lonely in a small town in the middle of nowhere, and at the age of eight, and with a love of nature and a nimble mind, Gary set out to read every book in the two-room Mano Public Library. Every afternoon and on weekends too, Gary checked out the maximum ten books and sat under a quiet table and studied subjects like architecture, biology, French, physics, and chemistry, and by the time he entered high school he was convinced that the key to preserving mankind's presence on earth was through the reduction of fossil fuels and reducing the greenhouse effect on the ozone layer.

Gary earned a scholarship to the state university, where he fell deeper in love with learning and joined every science-related club the school had to offer. He also fell in and out of love with a few of his classmates, having brief relationships that often devastated him when they came to a speedy end.

"You're kinda cute, Gary," one ex-lover told him as she explained why he was no longer welcome in her dorm room, "but you're too smart for your own damn good. You need to loosen up and learn how to have fun sometimes. Everything ain't always about an atom or a molecule, you know."

Battered but not broken, Gary took the advice to heart and began to cultivate several nonacademic interests. He studied jazz and learned to play the bass guitar. Always a bit self-conscious about his slight stature, he took up boxing and got his nose broken the first time in the ring. One of his frat brothers, Matthew Yarbridge, invited him to a secret Masonic meeting, and Gary was turned on by the rules and the rituals and was damn proud of himself when he survived the initiation.

It was during medical school that he'd met Felicia. They were attending a physics conference and a buzz was going up among some of the male doctors about the fine female intern who'd just registered for the conference that day.

Gary had smirked as some of his cocky colleagues practically knocked each other down to get her attention, and decided it was best to just keep his head in his notes. Standing five eight in shoes and weighing less than a buck fifty fully clothed, he wasn't exactly a jock, so he saw no need to throw himself into contention.

It was Felicia who had picked him from the crowd, and later they would laugh about that. She was a beautiful, striking woman and was accustomed to men of all races and ages tripping over each other in an attempt to gain her attention.

"My mother always said, 'Take a good look at the one who's doing the least amount of looking at you,'" she had laughed.

They'd gone to a funky little jazz club on the edge of town and shared a bottle of expensive wine. Felicia had gone up on stage and grabbed a microphone, and when she opened her mouth to sing, Gary had been stricken not only by Felicia's exquisite voice and physical beauty but also by the depth of her passion and the wonders of her mind.

Gary had shared that his mother was deceased but that he kept in close contact with his father, and Felicia revealed that her parents were both physicians and that she was the baby of the family. They danced closely and he tasted the sweetness of wine on her lips and wondered if she'd allow him to hold her for the next fifty years.

The conference was over far too soon, and Gary

headed back to New York where he was working for a publicly traded corporation, while Felicia flew to Chicago where her research position and a large clan of loving kin awaited her.

They began a long-distance relationship that consisted of cards, letters, and endless phone calls that always ended with Felicia singing the chorus to Minnie Riperton's "Lovin' You" before hanging up. *Lovin' you . . . has made my life so beautiful . . .*

It was a tense but exciting six months, that precious period of time Gary spent working up the nerve to propose to her. Expensive as hell too. He'd begun visiting her in Chicago every other weekend, and Gary should have purchased himself some airline stock as much flying back and forth as he was doing.

But while the bills took a big bite out of his pocket, they were nothing compared to what Felicia was doing to his heart. She was the kindest, funniest, smartest girl he had ever met, and being with her was well worth every penny Gary spent. Yet after asking Felicia's father for her hand, and then securing the blessings of her mother and four beautiful sisters, Gary had a pretty clear understanding of the enormous role and responsibility he would be undertaking by placing a ring on her finger.

"Son," Dr. Barrus Franklin had gripped Gary's hand and told him in a strong, no-nonsense voice, "Felicia's my baby and I love her. Don't take her nowhere and do her bad, you hear? I'll have to fuck you up. I mean that."

Barrus was a large, handsome man. His shoulders were wide enough for two men, and Gary had nearly cried out and fallen on his knees as the older man twisted his wrist up and bent his fingers back.

"In this family," Dr. Franklin had growled while applying enough pressure to make Gary pant and sweat, "we love our women. We respect them. We take *good care* of them. I've got five daughters and not one of them has to ever leave my house unless she wants to. You remember that, you hear?"

Gary had heard his future father-in-law loud and clear, and when he married Felicia Franklin on a sunny day in early June, he remembered the old man's words and swore to God and to himself that he would live up to them.

And he had. With every breath in his body, he had.

They'd found out pretty quickly that Felicia was infertile. Something was very wrong with the positioning of her uterus. She'd never be able to carry a child to full term. They'd considered other options; surrogacy, adoption. All were viable, but they were content as a couple and the matter was never that pressing.

The years passed and Gary and Felicia devoted themselves to their life's work and to loving each other. They traveled the globe together, both for research and for sheer pleasure. Early in their marriage Felicia had convinced him to do a short stint with the Peace Corps in Kenya, and two years later, after his good friend Matthew's wife died in childbirth and left him with two disabled daughters, Gary had signed him and Felicia both up as technical assistants for Doctors Without Borders to work with the physically disabled population in the Philippines.

He and Felicia lived well and harmoniously together, and with no children to prevent spontaneity, their sex life was off the radar. While during their period of dating Felicia had emerged as the bed champion with the stronger libido, it wasn't long after the wedding that Gary's demand caught up with his supply.

"I thought you said you only needed it twice a week!" Felicia panted as she wriggled her hips under his for the fourth time in as many days.

Gary had arched his back and dug in deeper. "I lied," he whispered and stroked harder.

"Besides . . . why need what you don't have?" He'd

groaned and withdrew from her tightness, then flipped her over and pulled her hips back and dove in again. "Now that I got it all the time . . . I need it all the time!"

And he'd gotten it all the time too. For thirty wonderful years Gary's wife had taken care of his every want and need, and when she became ill Gary had flung himself headlong into providing for her care.

In the beginning Felicia had still been able to work. She tired easily, so she went in each morning as usual, and was typically home for a nap by early afternoon. Her colleagues loved her and the staff she managed was loyal and devoted.

She and Gary were frank and open about her condition, and they both realized that her disease would soon progress to a point where her presence in a multimillion-dollar laboratory would be unsafe for her and for everyone else, but Gary was grateful for the patience and respect Felicia's coworkers showed her, and he was confident that they'd let him know when it was time for her to come home for good.

That notice had come much sooner than either he or Felicia had expected. Gary had received an emergency call from Ronald Naimone, one of Felicia's favorite lab techs, who informed him that Felicia had been intercepted trying to take a toxic sample out of a controlled area. He told Gary that Felicia had turned violent and verbally abusive when staff members tried to convince her to follow laboratory protocol and security procedures.

It was a sad day when Gary visited his wife's office alone and began packing up thirty years worth of her life's work. He'd called Felicia's sister, who had agreed to come spend the day with her while Gary closed the last chapter on his wife's professional career, and he wept as he removed plaques from her walls and boxed stacks of her awards and professional reviews.

Even at this stage Gary could still handle Felicia by himself at home. He'd taken a hiatus from work and devoted himself to caring for her around the clock, but caretaking was exhausting and he must have been sleeping extra hard late one night when Felicia crawled over him in bed and wandered out of the house. Gary had awakened in a panic when the door alarm had gone off and he'd opened his eyes to find his wife was no longer at his side, although he'd been careful to push the bed against the wall and use his body to box her in.

The entryway to their house fronted a very busy street, and lately the neighborhood hardheads had taken to drag racing up and down the street at all times of night, striking fear in other motorists and making enough noise to disturb the sleeping residents. With the alarm ringing in his ears, Gary had bolted from the room screaming Felicia's name, and the sight of the front door standing open to the night air nearly sunk him to the ground.

He ran outside and there she was, wearing the pink designer pajamas he had dressed her in and looking just as regal and beautiful as ever. Noting the look of confusion in her eyes, Gary had taken her into his arms and trembled with relief. Thank God she had only made it as far as the driveway, but the enormity of what might have happened struck him low in his heart, and the next morning Gary called a staffing agency and hired his wife a part-time health attendant.

Over the next few months Felicia's condition worsened rapidly, and even though Gary had tried to prepare himself for this stage of her illness, he quickly found that he was totally unprepared for any semblance of life without his wife. In short, he missed her. He missed their conversations, their fiercely competitive games of Scrabble, their intellectual battles over politics and the Sunday paper, and the late-night lovemaking sessions that had sustained their union for a solid three decades.

Sure, Felicia's body was still beside him each day, but the essence of who she was had gone. Occasionally he would catch a small glimpse of her fighting spirit in the tilt of her head or the rise of her smile, but more often than not there was nothingness inside of her, and when something intelligible did come from her it was usually an old, faded memory that had somehow pushed its way to the surface of her unstable, confused mind.

Never an overly emotional man, Gary found himself weeping uncontrollably several times each day. He missed his wife, but strangely enough he was also experiencing a strange yearning for his long-dead mother, and never before had his world felt so empty.

Felicia, in her wise and loving way, had known these trying days would come upon her man. She knew Gary was the kind of man who needed to feel a solid connection to someone central in his life, and while she was still clear-minded she had grieved for the pain and loneliness she knew her man would endure. Because she loved him, she'd forced him to talk about every scenario of her illness and the eventuality of her death. She'd begged him to continue living a rich life after her time on earth was gone, and she made him swear to her that he wouldn't close himself off to the rest of the world.

A researcher by nature and profession, Felicia had learned everything she could about the prognosis and progression of her disease. She knew there wouldn't be much time. She'd purchased a video camera and set about recording messages to Gary that he could find and view later, when he needed them, and she also purchased heartfelt cards and wrote long letters and short notes that she gave to a trusted friend with detailed instructions on when to mail them.

All in all, Gary and Felicia had kept the faith despite her disease. They'd taken the gift of love that God had granted them and enjoyed it to the fullest. They'd seen and done more than most people do in a lifetime, and contributed to the human race with their intellect and altruism. Scientifically, the Brownings viewed Felicia's tumor as something to be studied and death as a natural progression from life. They had done the best they could, made lemonade out of their lemons, and stood prepared to face the bad with the same love and determination that they had accepted the good.

Gary remembered that long-ago conversation he'd had with Barrus Franklin when the old man had damn near broken his wrist. In Gary's heart he truly believed that he'd lived every day of his thirty-year marriage in honor and service to his wife, and that knowledge sustained him through the long, cold nights as he lay alone in bed, missing her, missing the intimacy they'd once shared.

This knowledge was firm in his heart late one Tuesday night as Gary lay on the sofa surfing cable channels. He'd come home earlier in the evening after spending twelve hours by his wife's bedside, holding her limp hand and gazing into her empty eyes. Felicia was lingering and the doctors couldn't explain it. Most patients succumbed to the type of tumor she had in three to four months, but the brain is a wondrous and mysterious organ, and Felicia had been clinging to her physical life for close to a year. For the past six months there had been only sporadic bursts of conversation, and this morning's hoarse request for breakfast and the mention of a work project long past due had shaken Gary.

He'd taken a shower and gone to bed at his usual time, but had awakened just an hour or so later, unable to remain asleep. Munching on a few wheat crackers, he'd stretched out on the sofa and turned on the television, surfing mindlessly for something that might tamp down his sorrow and allow his heart a brief moment of peace.

He cruised past several of those simple-minded reality shows, a cooking channel, and a home-shopping network, then flicked the remote several times in succession to get past the barrage of cartoon channels that were catering to children in the middle of the night. Yawning, he settled on a cable channel where an old Bruce Lee rerun was showing. Stuffing a pillow under his head, Gary dug in and got comfortable. Long minutes passed and somehow he must have dozed off, because the next thing Gary knew he was awakening to a voice that was so amazing, so tantalizing, that it actually fondled him from the television set and enveloped him in a heart-warming cloud of comfort he hadn't experienced in almost a year.

"Felicia . . . ?" he muttered startled, then shook his head at the absurdity of it all.

The voice being emitted from the speakers was that of a songbird, but of course it wasn't Felicia. It was Felicia-like, though it was sweet and pure and alluring, and tears welled in Gary's eyes and his heart thudded in his chest as he listened to her.

A beautiful woman with long red hair and large breasts lounged on the screen, but what she looked like was irrelevant. The words she spoke were unimportant. What she advertised was meaningless to him. It was her voice that compelled him. The pitch that provoked him, and when she uttered a number Gary blinked a few times, then reached for the phone and began dialing without hesitation.

He dialed 1-900-A-N-Y-T-I-M-E.

• • •

Bliss's special client was one she didn't have to dress up for.

There was no fantasy to fulfill, no role playing to engage in, no whipped cream, chains, imaginary lovers, or dildos to ride.

He was the dress and heels type, and whenever Bliss prepared for his calls she pretended to be going on a dinner date with a dapper gentleman who would bring her beautiful fresh flowers and pull out her chair.

She turned on her laptop and flipped through the pages of her study guide as she waited for the computer to boot. She was an amazingly fast learner and had a photographic memory. She was planning to show her client a couple of new moves tonight, that was for sure. After logging on to the system, Bliss accessed what was fast becoming one of her favorite chat rooms and signed herself in just as the telephone rang.

"Hey, Gary," she greeted him after glancing at the caller ID and checking to make sure his credit card charge was approved. "What's happening?"

"Good evening, Bliss. The earth continues to rotate on its axis in my neck of the woods. How's life treating you?"

"Great. Everything on my end is great. I've been studying hard, I just want you to know that, okay? You ready to play?"

Gary laughed. He did that a lot when talking to Bliss.

"Just hold on, buckaroo. Let me get myself situated here."

"Yeah, get situated," Bliss teased. "Buckle your seat belt and check your pockets because I'm about to steal everything on your board."

Gary laughed again. "Oh shit, what have I done? I've created a monster and unleashed it on myself! Okay, okay, I'm logging into the room now. Get ready."

"Oh, I'm ready!"

"Okay, I'm in. You see me?"

"I see you. Call it!"

"No, ladies before gentlemen, you know that. Go ahead. Call it."

"Cool. Onyx before ivory. I'm black."

"Good choice. For tonight, I'm white."

"That's quite all right!"

For the next fifteen minutes Bliss put some moves on Gary that blew his mind. He'd introduced her to the game of chess and explained its fundamentals, but little did he know that Bliss took every opportunity to exercise her mind with all the seriousness she could muster. He'd given her a list of four beginner-level chess guides to order, and while she was on Amazon.com Bliss went ahead and ordered three advanced guides as well. Gary considered himself a fine chess player, and had competed in many tournaments during his younger years. And even though he'd cautioned Bliss not to read too far head in her lessons, Bliss had already read and consumed all seven guides and was planning to order a few more.

"Hey!" Gary exclaimed as Bliss outmaneuvered him and performed a complex king's gambit that primed her for an offensive attack. "Where'd you learn to do that?"

"Ahhh, you don't know *half* of what I can do!"

"I see . . ." Gary mused. "I see . . ."

Bliss mounted a Sicilian defense that left Gary scratching his head, and by the end of the call she had bested him in every game.

"Are you sure Bobby Fischer isn't over there sitting beside you?" Gary joked.

Bliss giggled. "Nope, I beat you all by myself. Plus that old guy is dead."

"Just thought I'd check," Gary said, and Bliss could tell he was smiling.

And she was happy about that. The first time she'd

taken a call from him had been quite an experience. Bliss had received her share of wacko calls when her line was public, and some of the requests she received were so outlandish that they weren't worth the money she made on the call.

But this guy was different. For one thing, he'd called in the middle of the night and the first thing he'd done was apologize for disturbing her.

"I'm sorry. I don't mean to bother you. I don't know what got into me, but I've never done this before and I'm not sure how it works."

Bliss had laughed sexily. "Well, it's supposed to work the same way every time, honey. You having a little problem that Bliss might help you fix?"

She was surprised as hell when he asked her if she could sing.

Hell yeah she could sing.

"Well, can you sing Minnie Ripperton's 'Lovin' You'?"

Bliss had torn it down for him a cappella.

She was halfway through the second verse when she realized her client was crying. Loud, wrenching tears that seemed to come straight from a devastated heart.

"Are you okay?" Bliss had asked, and immediately he'd begged her to continue.

"P-p-please. Sing, dear. I'll be fine. Just sing."

And sing Bliss did. She sang Gary right into the first peaceful sleep he'd had in months.

Over the next few weeks Gary called her sporadically, always with the same request. "Sing Minnie Riperton's 'Lovin' You.'"

Bliss was puzzled. Gary wasn't interested in what she looked like and had never once mentioned sex. There were no kinky requests, no S & M fantasies, and no desperate sounds of masturbation spurred by the mental images Bliss was expected to create in her clients' minds.

The only thing Gary seemed to want from her was conversation. Whether it was on current events, global warming, the laws of antigravity, or the plight of AIDS orphans in Africa, Gary seemed to appreciate Bliss for the keenness of her intellect, and his only requirement was that she sing to him at the conclusion of their calls.

"Tell me," she'd asked during one such call when she couldn't take it anymore. "I love singing to you, Gary, really I do. But you can download 'Lovin' You' from iTunes and play it as much as you like, you know? I run a sex line, yet you don't seem interested in sex. Why do you call me?"

Gary had hesitated for a long moment then

responded, "My wife is sick. She has a terminal illness and she's dying. I would never cheat on her. I'm not that kind of man. But she used to sing to me when she was well. 'Lovin' You' was our song. I get lonely sometimes. Really sad too. I have no real family. Felicia and I couldn't have any children and I was an only child. I just like talking to you, Bliss. You're more alive than Minnie Ripperton. Listening to you sing brings my wife back to life."

And on that note, Bliss opened her mouth and let the gift God had blessed her with fly out. She pretended to be Felicia as she sang to Gary. She sang not like a sick woman who was lying in bed dying but like a woman in love who was serenading her man.

On the other end Gary wept.

Cradling the phone in his hands he felt his wife's love coursing through his veins, and at that moment he knew that Felicia's body would very soon follow her mind. His wife didn't have long in this physical world, but listening to Bliss sing, he knew that Felicia's spirit—and her song— would live with him forever.

CHAPTER 9

SALLY Godfrey was in love with the law.

From as far back as she could remember she'd dreamed of either litigating in a courtroom or championing some aspect of the law, and during her college days she'd studied trial notes and read case law while everyone else was out partying until the sun came up.

And all of her hard work and sacrifices had paid of grandly too. For the past eight years Sally had worked as a state legislator, enacting laws that kept women and children safe in her city. She'd fought hard to tighten residency restrictions for convicted child molesters and had furiously championed legislation calling for harsher punishment for men who were caught soliciting or engaging in prostitution.

A well-loved figure in middle Tennessee social and professional circles, Sally was married to the handsome Joe Godfrey, a highly regarded fast-tracking district attorney who was said to be a shoo-in for the office of mayor one day. They'd had a whirlwind public romance and become the darlings of society columnists from coast to coast.

Both Godfreys were brilliantly intense, with sharp legal minds that amazed their colleagues and opponents alike. It wasn't unusual for them to work fifteen hours a day and bring legal briefs home with them to study long into the night as well, and Sally thought it was cute on those long, exhausting nights when she and Joe both fell asleep with paperwork scattered between them in the bed.

But as hard as they worked on their careers, the Godfreys also relished their limited private time together and often took mini-vacations at the drop of a hat, just to get away from their grueling schedules and to recharge their emotional batteries. They'd vacationed in Alaska, France, Thailand, Africa, and several other exotic paradises around the globe. Joe was a passionate and attentive husband. A generous lover who spared no expense or favor on his beautiful, younger wife. He lavished her with gifts, treated her like a queen, and respected her as an intellectual equal, and Sally knew that tens of thousands of other women would walk across hot coals just to be in her position.

But life hadn't always been so sweet for Sally Godfrey. Back in the days when she was still Sally Andrews, she'd spent her formative years in Fort Bragg, North Carolina, the daughter of a military man and a registered nurse. The youngest of three fair-haired, blue-eyed girls, Sally was an identical twin to her sister Shayna, and while the girls looked alike down to the tiny mole near the bottom of their left earlobes, they were polar opposites in almost every other way.

Whereas Sally was a shy but brilliant and unassuming youngster, Shayna was a fidgety maverick who looked for opportunities to disobey their ultra-rigid father and disgrace their family name.

Colonel James Andrews ran his household in much the same manner as he ran his military outfit. With extreme discipline and stark attention to detail. His oldest daughter, Samantha, was tasked to sit for her sisters during the hottest days of summer while both the colonel and his wife were at work, and it was all Samantha and Sally could do together to keep the rebellious Shayna in check.

All three Andrews girls had beautiful figures and were very early bloomers, and while Samantha and Sally wore clothing appropriate for their ages and levels of maturity, Shayna began stealing sexy clothing from local department stores at the age of twelve, and no matter what cute, carefully ironed little girly short set she was wearing when her parents left for work each morning, it sure as hell wasn't what she flounced out of the house in a couple of hours later as she ran off to meet as much trouble as she could find.

"Don't you want a boyfriend?" Shayna had asked one morning as her twin sat cross-legged on her bed staring at what had just come in the mail.

"No," Sally had answered truthfully. She had absolutely no interest in boys. "Not really."

"Well, I do," Shayna had said, lifting a glass dildo out of a plain box. "Look at what I ordered. Wanna try it out first, Sally?"

Sally had recoiled. She had her desires, but sticking something hard and long inside of her wasn't one of them.

"No, Shayna. I don't."

"It's just a dick," Shayna had teased. "Dad sticks his inside Mom all the time."

"Shayna, cut it out!" Samantha tried to exert her

limited authority as her younger sister sprawled in their father's chair with the dildo stuffed between her legs. She stared in disbelief as Shayna lit one of their father's cigarettes, then drank some of his vodka straight from the bottle. Colonel Andrews was a firm believer in mass punishment. When one girl stepped out of line, all three of them got slapped back in. And if she stepped out too far, his wife got slapped back in line right along with them. Samantha was fearful of this. "Put that thing away before you end up getting all of us in trouble!"

But Shayna didn't give a damn about trouble. In fact, she seemed to live for it and did her best to get the biggest rise out of their parents that she could.

By the time she was fourteen Shayna was cutting school regularly to drink and smoke weed with older boys from the local high school. She'd been having unprotected sex for so long that she'd had two secret abortions that nobody knew about except Samantha and Sally.

While Samantha loved her sisters, she feared her father, and her main concern was that Shayna not get caught doing anything that the colonel might make all of them pay for. At seventeen Samantha had a boyfriend of her own, and though she'd taken a few drinks and had been caught experimenting with drugs once or twice, she was nowhere as bold as her younger sister, and she loved her mother enough to keep her own vices to a minimum.

But Sally loved everybody.

She was a good girl who didn't like making waves or causing pain. It scared her half to death when Shayna snuck out of bed in the middle of the night to run off and party with the boys in town. She could only imagine the risqué things her twin sister did while she was out there on the streets, and Sally was terrified that something bad would happen and Shayna might get hurt and never come back home.

On nights like those Sally would climb into Shayna's vacated bed and inhale her sister's scent from her pillow, praying fervently for God to bring her twin home safely. And hours later, when Shayna would finally drag herself in just before dawn reeking of alcohol, cigarettes, and the bodies of countless unwashed men, Sally would lie there clinging to her sister as Shayna told her about all the naughty things she'd done and how she couldn't wait to do them all again.

Time passed, and Sally found a friend in a red-headed girl named Maria who was visiting her father for the summer. The house next door had been renovated and divided into three apartments, and Maria's father was a tenant in the smallest one. For the first time in her life Sally had someone who understood who she was on the deepest levels, and hanging out with Maria on the porch behind her house became a wonderful thing. They spent every free moment together, taking long walks, giggling, sharing secrets. They found a shady spot under the awning where they lay down together and whispered and hugged and touched, and at those times, gyrating slowly on top of Maria with their budding breasts pressed together, Sally was the happiest girl in the whole world.

Maria was only required to spend one month with her father during summer visits, and on the afternoon that she left to fly back to her mother in California, Sally's mom had come home from her shift at the hospital early, red in the face and livid.

"What on earth is wrong with you?" She'd burst into the house and screamed at Shayna in unparalleled disgust. "Our neighbor Mrs. Payton just called my job! She said she saw you lying on top of a girl on our back porch!"

"That's a lie!" Shayna had yelled right back.

"No, Shayna, it's the truth! She *saw* you! You had your shorts down! She said you were lying on top of some girl and *kissing* her, Shayna! Why are you behaving this way? What kind of horrible things are you doing to yourself?"

Filled with shame, Sally had run into her bedroom and hidden her face in her hands, and when their father came home and found out what Shayna had supposedly done, for the first time in his life Colonel Andrews had taken off his military belt and used it on one of his daughters.

"You filthy child!" he said, his chin quivering with rage. "Hold still. You need to be punished."

But Shayna had refused to submit to the whipping, no matter how fast the colonel let his belt fly.

"Admit what you've done, Shayna. Admit it!"

Mortified, Sally had sat hugging her knees on the floor as her sister took the brutal blows in silence. She covered her face with her hands and the scent of Maria's body, still coating her fingers from the intimate goodbye games they'd played on the back porch, flooded her nose.

"Promise me, Shayna! Promise you'll never do anything like that again!"

"I promise!" Sally screamed as Shayna silently enduring the beating. "I won't do it again!"

"*No*, Sally!" their father had barked over his broad shoulder. "Don't *you* say it! Don't you try to save her. This time let this devil take her *own* due!"

Spank! Spank! Spank!

When it was finally over and their father had left the room sweating, Sally could barely meet her sister's eyes. Shayna's skin was bruised and welted all along her arms and legs, and it was obviously very painful for her to move.

"Its okay, Sally," Shayna said as she rose and hobbled over to reach for her sister, who still cried pitifully on the floor. Shayna hugged Sally to her breast and kissed her twin's sweaty forehead. "I understand you, and everything's going to be okay."

If the good colonel thought he had cured Shayna of something deviant with his belt whipping, he was sorely mistaken. The beating seemed to release something dark in the girl, to bring out the absolute worst in her. She doubled her drinking and flaunted her cigarette smoking in her mother's face. She hooked up with a young private from the base and began sneaking into the male barracks at night.

It was only a matter of time before the colonel got wind of what was going on with his middle daughter. Shayna had been absent from school enough days to be classified as a truant, and the lower-enlisted men on post were also starting to talk.

After formation one morning the colonel was handed a letter from one of his soldiers that spelled out things about his daughter he could have gone without knowing. According to the note, Shayna had spent a particularly wild drunken night in the barracks being passed around to whoever wanted her, and the sordid acts that the remorseful young soldier described being performed on Shayna were enough to make her heartbroken father retreat into his office and weep.

That was the last straw for the Andersons. Shayna was packed up and sent four hours south to a rehabilitative school for at-risk young girls, and the morning Shayna left Sally had the strangest premonition that she would never see her sister again.

The feeling was so intense that her father had to drag Sally from the car before he could drive off with her twin, and she'd fought and screamed and made such a scene in the front yard that all the neighbors came out to watch.

In the end, Shayna had waved good-bye from the back window as Sally shook with grief in their mother's arms. Not more than a month later, the eldest girl, Samantha, would defy their father and run off and marry her thirty-five-year-old airman boyfriend, who was being reassigned to Texas, and six weeks later their mother would be diagnosed with breast cancer.

It was a turbulent time for Sally, and for her father as

well. The loss of two daughters and his wife's life-threatening illness nearly crippled the fierce, imposing man. To top it off, he'd stopped taking the medication he'd been prescribed to help combat his post-traumatic stress disorder, and he'd become depressed and erratic.

Sally responded to this new crisis by being extra-good. She was loath to cause her parents an additional ounce of grief, so she was on her best behavior and did the right thing at all times.

The colonel recognized her efforts and was highly pleased with his youngest child. "Thank God you're nothing like your sisters, darling. Your mother and I can actually *trust* you. Your heart is pure. You're a *good* girl, Sally." Her father would pat her arm and declare with a look of pure gratitude in his eyes. "A good, *good* girl."

And she was. Sally went to school each day and studied hard. She registered for her SATs and began scouring the Internet to apply to suitable colleges. At home, she cooked, cleaned, starched her father's shirts, and sat up with her mother at night as she grew weak from chemotherapy. As a sign of love and allegiance, Sally shaved her head when her mother's beautiful locks began falling out in clumps, and she designed a T-shirt for her mother that read, "I have cancer—it does NOT have me!"

During her last two years of high school Sally did her best to be a far better daughter than either of her sisters had been, and the sheer gratitude and relief that her parents expressed was more than enough compensation for her.

"You're a *good* girl, Sally," her father never stopped reminding her. "A good, *good* girl."

Nearly three years after driving Sally's wayward twin Shayna south, the now-retired colonel received a devastating telephone call from a police station in a big city in Colorado.

The news was bad. His middle daughter had been found dead.

Shayna had died of a drug overdose and her body was being held at the local coroner's office. It was a tragic ending to a short, tragic life. Shayna had lasted less than a week in the group home the colonel had signed her into. Instead of being rehabilitated, she'd searched for the local drug haunts and gotten hooked on methamphetamines, and shortly thereafter she began selling her body on the streets to support her new habit.

The Andrews family was devastated. Samantha and her husband had come home from Texas and they'd all grieved together as Shayna was laid to rest in a local cemetery.

"When do you leave for college?" Samantha had asked Sally the day after Shayna's funeral. Samantha was packing her clothing and preparing for the trip home she would take with her husband later in the day.

"I don't think I'm going. At least not this year. Maybe I'll get a job on base or something. You know, so I can stay close to Mom and Dad."

"What you should do is get the hell out of here," Samantha had balked. "Mom and Dad made their own choices and lived their own lives, Sally. Save yourself. Leave. Don't hang around here just because of them."

Sally had been appalled.

"After everything Mom and Dad have been through? After losing Shayna, losing you, Mom being sick . . . you think I could just abandon them like that?"

Samantha had shrugged. "It's your life, Sally. You have a right to it. Shayna never let anybody hold her back from doing what she wanted—"

"Yeah, and look at where we left Shayna yesterday too," Sally scoffed. "In a lonely grave out in a cemetery that nobody but me will probably ever visit."

"But it was *her* life," Samantha argued. "She decided for herself what shape it would take. You have to do the same thing, Sally. You owe it to yourself."

You're a good girl, Sally. A good, good girl.

On some levels Sally agreed with her sister. She wanted so badly to leave North Carolina behind and run off to college. But her mother's cancer had recently returned, this time in her lymph nodes, and each time Sally thought of leaving home she suffered such severe bouts of guilt that her head would ache and she'd almost pass out.

Even her father's hopes were a source of extreme stress. Sally had received scholarship offers from several solid schools, and her parents were proud of her and anxious to find out which would be her choice.

"Where to, Sally?" her father asked every other day. "C'mon, dear. You've got a great pool to choose from. Did you pick one yet?"

It had broken the colonel's heart when she finally blurted out, "I'm not going to school, Dad! How the hell do you expect me to go to school when Mom is sick and you're sick, and there's nobody left around here to be good except *me?*"

The look on her father's face had crushed her heart and Sally had quickly apologized. The colonel had hugged her and kissed her hair and told Sally how much he and her mother loved her and how badly they wanted her to have a wonderful future, a wonderful life. The colonel made Sally promise that she would look closely at her scholarship offers, then choose a school and to stick with her choice.

"We love you, Sally," he told her. "Every single thing about you is pure."

You're a good girl, Sally. A good, good *girl.*

As it turned out, the decision was taken out of her hands.

Weeks earlier Sally had applied for a job at the bowling alley on post, and the day after talking to her father, the site manager called her in for an interview. To Sally's surprise, the woman waiting to interview her was the mother of a good friend from school.

"Sally Andrews! I can't believe you're here! When I saw your application I thought there must be some mistake, perhaps something you had applied for over the summer that was just now finding its way to my desk!"

Sally had smiled ruefully. "Hello, Mrs. Dobson. How's Cathy?"

"She's doing great." Mrs. Dobson beamed. "She's getting ready for college and growing more excited by the day. She got her roommate assignment yesterday, a girl from California, and they've been talking on the phone nonstop."

Sally smiled again, hiding her jealousy. She sat with

her eyes downcast as her friend's mother peered at her closely.

"Look, Sally, I just got this position a few months ago, and the only reason I took it is because with Cathy going off to school there'll be a whole lot less for me to do around the house. But I thought you were going to college too, Sally? You're such a great student and Cathy told me about all the scholarship offers you received. Why would you turn all of that down to work here in the bowling alley?"

It had taken more control than Sally knew she had, but she fought her tears and refused to cry.

You're a good girl, Sally. A good, good girl.

Instead she shrugged. "College is still an open option for me, Mrs. Dobson. I've just decided to take a year off to figure out what it is that I really want to do."

"Oh," the woman said kindly. "I understand. How's your mother, Sally? I've been meaning to give her a call but it never seems to be the right time."

"She's fine." Sally shrugged, fighting against her tears harder than ever. "My mom is doing just fine."

Ten minutes later Sally had walked out of the bowling alley with a red apron and a new job. Mrs. Dobson had instructed her to return the following Monday at nine sharp to begin her training.

The drive home from base was a blur, with Sally wiping her eyes frequently in order to see the road. Just for once she wished she had the courage to do something selfish. To say to hell with everyone else and be bad. She'd spent her high school years taking care of her mother and catering to her father. Instead of dating and partying and exploring some of the things she really wanted to learn about herself, she'd pushed her needs to the back of her mind and concentrated on being a good girl.

Just once Sally would have liked to smoke a joint, steal from a convenience store, or do something forbidden . . . with someone forbidden. But Shayna and Samantha had done so much, had caused so much pain, that there was no room for Sally to deviate from the norm. Sometimes the selfish, racy thoughts that filled Sally's mind flooded her with guilt. Her parents put her on a pedestal, and she had vowed not to be like her sisters.

Torn between her right to her own future and her duty to her parents, Sally drove up to the small home that she shared with her parents, surprised to see that her father's car was gone from the driveway.

Sally was alarmed. The colonel had been suffering horrible flashbacks and vivid nightmares, and a few weeks earlier Sally had awakened to find him standing in her doorway holding a pistol in his hand.

"Dad? Is everything okay?"

"Everything is fine, darling. You're a *good* girl, you know, Sally. A good, *good* girl."

"Dad?" Sally had bolted from the bed. "What are you doing with that gun? Where's Mom?"

"Settle down," Colonel Andrews had told his daughter. "Your mother is fine."

Sally had taken the gun from her father's hand and led him back to bed. Her mother had been sleeping peacefully, and Sally had taken the handgun and stashed it in the basement behind an old box of Shayna's clothes.

Her father's emotional state was getting progressively worse. Sally was worried about him, about her mother too, but she was at a loss as to what to do.

And now, walking toward her house, the missing car frightened her.

Sally's mother was too weak to be moved, and someone had to be at home with her at all times. Her father hadn't mentioned any VA or doctor's appointment before Sally left for her interview, and it was inconceivable that the colonel had left his wife at home alone.

The house was quiet as Sally entered and she called

out her mother's name from the doorway. Rushing toward the master bedroom, Sally was shocked to find the bed empty.

She tried to rationalize. It was obvious that her parents were out somewhere together. But had something happened? If her mother had had an emergency then her father would have called 911. But if he had called 911 then he would have ridden in the ambulance with his wife. So where was his car?

Sally walked slowly into the kitchen, and the moment her eyes settled on the small sheet of paper bearing her father's precise, block handwriting, she knew. With trembling fingers she picked up the single page that had her name written at the top and began to read.

Sally,

Your mother and I are at the railroad crossing near Nature Creek. Please go away to college, dear. You're a smart, beautiful young lady and the best daughter any parent could have. I'm sorry we had to leave you, but neither of us wanted to be a burden. You have your whole life ahead of you, my darling. Please live it. You're a good, good girl, Sally. A good girl.

See you in heaven,

Dad and Mom

Sally sat quietly in her father's chair until there was a knock at the door. She didn't think and she didn't cry. When the state troopers came in and informed her that her father's car had stalled at a railroad crossing and been hit by a train, the tears finally fell, coming down in a torrent.

She left for Princeton the day after her parents' funeral. The house and the heirlooms and all her parents' personal effects she left for her sister Samantha to dispose of as she wished. Sally knew she'd never get over the death of her twin or the death of her parents, but would also never forget the ultimate sacrifice that had been made, no matter how devastating it was, on her behalf.

But as traumatic as her early life had been, the next fifteen years were magical for Sally. She'd met and married Joe at a time when she was ripe for a relationship, and almost every bad thing about her past had been buried deeply in her subconscious.

Today, Sally's life was enviable and storied, and there were many times that she thanked her lucky stars and knocked on wood to assure her continued favor. But deep inside, on the far peripherals of her emotions, there was still that strange yearning she'd explored only once at the age of fifteen. A yearning that neither Joe, her frenzied work, her social activities, nor her political and legal aspirations could fill.

You're a good girl, Sally. A good, good *girl.*

For years Sally had fought desperately against this yearning, viewing it as an aberration that deeper prayer and more bountiful good works could somehow wash from her heart. And for many years she'd done well, fighting this secret shameful thing in silence and in private, wondering why in the world such thoughts and desires continued to creep up on her unbidden, frightening her to tears and sullying her spirit.

There was absolutely nothing lacking in her life with Joe. He was great in bed, had more than an adequate hunk of equipment, gave head just as joyously as he received it, and made her sexual gratification his priority nearly every time they made love.

But Sally couldn't help the unnatural thoughts that flooded her mind, or the desires that flooded her body. Her fantasies were vivid and compelling. The yearning she fought was deep and demanding.

Sally knew all about sexual deviance. Her work brought her in close contact with some of the most depraved members of society. From pedophiles to prostitutes, Sally despised them all, and the main thrust of her life's work had gone toward eradicating these deviants from her community by imposing the harshest punishments against them allowable under the law.

But how could she punish the thing that dwelled within her? She felt awful even thinking about it, but that didn't stop her from wanting it. And six months earlier, while at a conference in Missouri, Sally's weaknesses had caught up with her and she had finally given in. It had been a long, hectic day filled with lectures and panel discussions, and back in her hotel room she'd been unable to sleep.

She'd already called Joe to say good night and was channel surfing when she came upon a pay-per-view station that immediately caught her attention. Just reading the tagline descriptions made Sally's body grow hot, and alone in the big soft bed her fingers wandered between her legs and she found sweet wetness there.

All hotel movies were billable to the guest's room, and since Sally was there on official business there was no way she could indulge herself by ordering one. Instead, she flipped through the channels and was stricken when a commercial advertisement flashed across the screen, where the most sensuous, silky voice was calling out a telephone number and promising to demonstrate the caller's secret fantasies in great detail.

Sally's mouth had watered at the sound of the voice

being emitted from the television speakers. It wasn't hard to read between the lines, as the woman promised to indulge—in just one call—all the delicious fantasies that Sally had been yearning to experience for so many years.

She had reached across the nightstand to grab a pencil, then realized that she didn't even need one. The number Sally was about to call was easy to remember and would soon prove impossible to forget.

It was 1-900-A-N-Y-T-I-M-E.

"I need a bottom bitch."

"I'm a bottom," Bliss answered, her voice low and submissive.

"I don't like this room. Let's go in another."

Bliss was on it. "Do you like the metal room? The chains have been oiled and the whips are properly hung. Will that be okay?"

There was a period of silence on the other end, and Bliss knew it was a toss-up which way the call would go. This was one conflicted-ass client. Sometimes the chick was so hot Bliss could barely answer the phone before she was getting toe-fucked by the client's pointy biker boot. Other times the voice on the other end of the line froze up the moment Bliss said hello, guilt seeming to dry up the woman's juices before she could get her words out.

"Did you color your hair?"

"No," Bliss answered softly. "I'm a sexy biker chick, and I always wear it short and flaming red. It matches the hair on my pussy. You wanna see it?"

"I don't have to see it. I can smell it."

"I'm wearing the spiked heels you like. The orange pair. I'm in my leather chaps and vest too. With nothing underneath."

"Pass me the hairbrush then go stand in the middle of the room."

Bliss pretended to do so on her end. "I'm there."

"Bend over. Grab your ankles."

"Oh," Bliss mewed softly. "Please don't . . . hurt . . ."

"Shut the fuck up! Lick my toes!"

Bliss made smacking noises as she licked and sucked the fingers on her left hand.

"Now take your punishment."

"Please," she begged.

Bliss heard the sound of flesh being spanked and the client moaned then cried out.

"You deserve that, don't you? You had your fingers in a bad place and you deserve to be spanked."

"Please," Bliss whispered, and despite herself she felt her pussy filling up with warm juice. "I deserve it, but please don't spank me again. I'll be good. I promise."

The spanking sound came again, and Bliss and her client both shuddered.

"You're supposed to be a *good* girl! A good, *good* girl! But you've been bad, you filthy little bitch. Hold your legs open. You need to be punished inside your thighs."

Bliss's thighs fell apart on the bed and her nipples hardened.

"I won't do it again. I promise. Please don't . . ."

Spank! Spank! Spank!

Bliss felt every delicious blow as the client brought the hairbrush down on the tender insides of her own thighs. Her skin tingled with pleasure-pain and she arched her back and cried out unintelligibly into the phone.

"Do you promise not to do those nasty things again?"

"I promise!" Bliss shrieked. "I promise!"

"Do you promise to be a *good* girl?"

Whop! Moan. *Spank!* Moan. Guttural groan, then a long, long sigh. The client had climaxed, but Bliss knew there was plenty more left where that had come from.

"The next time I catch you playing in Maria's panties I'll beat the life out of you, do you hear me?"

"Yes! I hear you! I promise!"

Bliss played along as the client directed her closer to the imaginary wall where the whips and chains were kept.

"I can feel you watching me as I walk," Bliss teased. "You love my long, willowy legs and my tight little bum, don't you?"

"I want to fuck you. Where's my peter?"

Bliss almost laughed. She'd heard it called some of everything. A johnson, a willie, a papi, a jimmy . . . not many of her clients called it a peter, but this one always did.

"It's right here," Bliss said quickly. "Strap it on tight and I'll raise my ass high in the air so you can get a good hit."

"Oh, God," the client moaned as she mentally penetrated Bliss and they started to get it on.

Bliss thrashed around on the bed, purposely hitting the headboard against the wall and making the springs creak loudly.

"I am *fucking* you, Maria! Your pussy is so wet and deep. You are such a *good* girl! I am fucking the *shit* out of you!"

Bliss agreed, stifling a giggle. "Yes, you are. Your peter is at least a meter! Deeper, baby. It's so hard, so long, so good!"

"Turn over. I want to suck your nipples."

Bliss made a big loud production on the bed, as though she was flipping over.

"My thirty-six D's are pointing north, just waiting for you. Oh, your tongue feels so good on them! Put it in. Please put it back in, hon. I need your peter, right now. I need you to fuck me like a *man!*"

They rocked together for the next fifteen minutes. They played with nipple clamps and rubbed coke on each other's clits. The client demanded that Bliss pinch and punish her nipples in ways that didn't seem pleasurable but produced multiple orgasms that made her scream into the phone.

Bliss wasn't all that into sexing women, but she wasn't against it, either. She got her share of pleasure from the fantasy, as she always did, and by the time the call ended she'd had a peter thrust into every orifice on her body and had even been handcuffed to a wall and lashed across the ass with a barbed leather belt.

Back during the days when Bliss had an open line, she'd serviced plenty of women who were bi-curious, so she'd incorporated a variety of girl-on-girl themes into their fantasies as a way of finding out what sex with a woman could be like. But this client, the one who insisted upon being referred to as Shayna even though the name on her credit card said Sally, and who always called her Maria instead of Bliss, was the only woman she'd kept on after going private, and there was something painful about the way she choked up during some of their encounters that was touching.

Of course, nearly all of her clients used her to satisfy needs and urges they couldn't or wouldn't satisfy in their real lives, and almost none of them went around broadcasting the fact that they were regulars on a phone sex line, but Miss Shayna seemed especially at odds with her sexual desires, which for some strange reason served to endear her to Bliss in a special way.

It was close to noon and Bliss was tiring. She was "seeing" Jim Burgess again later in the afternoon, but right now all she wanted to do was stretch out on her living room sofa and doze or watch reruns for a few hours. Once again, the makeup came off, as did the fake silver-studded tongue ring and the clip-on chain-linked earrings. Pulling at the snaps on the black leather riding suit she'd purchased from an erotic website, Bliss hung up her costume, wrapped herself in a soft, fluffy towel, and retreated from the Purple Room and into the sanctity of her tiny apartment.

CHAPTER 10

THE problem with rumors, Lattrell knew, was that denying them only pumped them up bigger and helped them spread faster.

That little bitch Phe-Nom had shit on Lattrell's rep, and the rap world was buzzing with all kinds of crazy speculations and innuendos that La-Rule was an ass-raider and had got caught bending over for some guy named Reggie.

Lattrell had almost shit on himself when Phe-Nom had banged on his dressing room door and busted him in a threesome with Bliss and Neck.

"Man who the fuck is up in there with *you?*" Phe-Nom had screamed, his voice high pitched and incredulous.

Lattrell had dropped the phone and scrambled into

his pants in two seconds flat. He opened the door panting and sweating, his ass still throbbing from the imaginary banging he'd just taken.

He stood there shirtless, the top button on his jeans still open.

"What you talking about, man?"

Phe-Nom had craned his neck, peering around Lattrell from all angles as he tried to see if someone else was in the room.

"Who's Reggie? Which Reggie you with? Reggie-B from Harlem? You got that nigga in here?"

Lattrell balked. "Man what you talking about? Ain't no Reggie-B in here! I don't even hang with that dude. Ain't *nobody* in here but me. What? You see somebody else? You see a ghost?"

Phe-Nom shrugged, grinning. "Nah, I don't see nobody but I heard you, man. You and some Reggie banger. It's cool, though. You do what you do, man. I ain't in your business."

Lattrell towered over the smaller man, flexing his massive muscles.

"Then what the fuck did you come down here for? Didn't they tell you the rules? I chill by *myself* after shows, man. Nobody disturbs me. You got that? *Nobody.*"

Phe-Nom shrugged again. His eyes crawled all over

the small room like he was taking mental pictures. "My bad, man. I didn't know. I came to see if you wanted to catch a ride. I got a fresh limo waiting outside. We got some honeys and we're going to the club. I thought you might wanna ride."

Lattrell nodded and played it cool. His mind was churning a thousand miles a minute. Phe-Nom was definitely going to run his mouth. As loud as he could run it. Lattrell always went to the club after a show. If he changed up his routine now he would look like he was ducking and hiding from something. The best thing he could do was stay cool. Act normal. Do what was expected of him just like he always did.

"Hell yeah I wanna ride." He reached on the floor for his belt and shirt.

"Your phone, man." Phe-Nom pointed at the cell phone lying open and still lit up under the glass coffee table where Lattrell had flung it. "Don't wanna forget that."

Lattrell bent and scooped up the phone up in his hand and snapped it shut. He was pulling his shirt over his head when Phe-Nom said, "Hey, I gotta pee. Can I use your bathroom, man?"

Lattrell shrugged and stayed easy.

"It's right there. Knock it out."

He watched as Phe-Nom disappeared into the small

restroom. While he was in there Lattrell hoped he'd check the medicine cabinet, under the sink, and behind the shower curtain too. There was no doubt that Phe-Nom was going to put him on blast, and although this was the worst possible thing that could happen in Lattrell's life, he was already preparing himself for the massive damage control he knew would have to be done.

Phe-Nom had given Lattrell a big headache.

Not only did he get on myspace.com, mediatakeout .com, suite101.com, and facebook.com, and put out gay bulletins about the hottest rapper on the charts, he even claimed rapper Reggie-B from Harlem, a known killer with ties to the Mafia, was his secret boner.

Lattrell's entourage reacted just the way he knew they would. Every last one of them ate off his profits, and they were ready to go after Phe-Nom and cut him at the throat.

"Why even acknowledge some bullshit like that?" Lattrell said, staying cool and trying to calm them down. The last thing he wanted was a war. He had beaten himself up over this thing day and night until he was worn down to a gristle.

His main concern wasn't that his fans might turn on him, which was a big possibility. It had happened to other top rappers whose sexuality was considered suspect, and it never failed that even though some people claimed that what grown people did behind closed doors was their own damned business, the real deal always showed in declining album sales.

Keeping Reggie-B off his ass for real was another concern that kept Lattrell sweating too. He'd heard through the grapevine that Reggie-B was psycho mad behind his name getting dragged through some nigga's shitty behind, and everybody knew when Reggie-B got mad there was no telling what kind of craziness that dude might try.

All that aside, there was something else that worried Lattrell more than the fans and Reggie-B combined.

His family.

As a minister, Lattrell's father didn't approve of his rap ideology or of the words he used in public, or of all the half-naked girls that hung off his arm. He refused to take a dime Lattrell offered him and forbid his wife to accept any of that devil's money, either. But unlike before, for the past several years Reverend Johnson had at least looked at his son with consideration in his eyes. Gone was that searching stare, the one Lattrell knew was ever ready to climb in the ring with any demon that might still prowl in his son's soul. Lattrell was grateful and relieved that the look of shame and disgust that had lurked in his father's eyes had been replaced with the basic respect that one man showed another, even when one was a sinner and the other a saint.

And this was the primary concern that drove Lattrell to commit to doing whatever it took to make sure he completely covered his tracks. Of course Phe-Nom hadn't busted him with anyone in his trailer, as he'd boasted all over the Internet. That dumb ass had looked everywhere except the microwave trying to find out who had been in that dressing room ass-raiding Lattrell.

The absolute certainty that nothing could ever be proven, that no man could ever step forward and make a claim on him gave Lattrell immeasurable relief. There had only been one time since the afternoon of his brother Javon's wedding and his entire community's laying on of hands that Lattrell had slipped up. Only once, and the memory of it still burned in Lattrell's heart.

It had gone down so fast and furious that it left Lattrell stunned and dismayed. He'd been in his man Spoil's home studio working on some beats. They'd smoked a whole tree of Trinny blue and swigged a couple of cases of Coronas. One minute they were jamming and getting nice, and the next thing Lattrell knew they were fucking like crazy and he was taking big meat.

It was so wild and Lattrell was so high that after it

was over and they were both back in their clothes drinking and smoking and talking about music and what was going on in the industry, he almost couldn't believe it had actually happened.

The fear of being found out had haunted Lattrell for weeks. His name was just beginning to catch fire and his label was putting more and more money into his promotions. Spoil didn't have nothing to lose. He was just a low-level producer and he could actually make a name off banging Lattrell's ass because he wasn't that well known and his beats weren't all that great.

Lattrell sat around on pins and needles wondering if that nigger Spoil was gonna drop a dime that he'd bent him over. And then out of nowhere his problem got solved. Spoil was hanging out with some rappers in Atlanta when they got robbed for their jewels. Spoil hesitated in giving up his goods and got shot in the head, and died right there on the sidewalk before the ambulance could even be called.

Lattrell had been raised a Christian and he didn't wish no bad luck on nobody, but he wasn't exactly sad to see Spoil go, either. Dead men told no tales, and that one crazy-ass-damned-good night in Spoil's studio was something Lattrell believed he and Spoil should both take to their graves.

And that brought him back to Phe-Nom and his current headache. There had been no quick furtive or forbidden sex to speak of, and Lattrell knew he couldn't count on Phe-Nom getting robbed and killed. There was nothing to trace any of his unnatural activities back to him. Nothing to tie him to anything that looked remotely unclean.

Except one thing.

Lattrell paid a visit to his accountant's office and retrieved every telephone and credit card bill he'd received over the past year. He'd sat alone in front of the fireplace in his living room and watched the evidence of his late nights with Bliss and Neck turn to ashes before his eyes. When the embers had died down Lattrell stretched out on the sofa and slept the best sleep he'd had in days.

But in the middle of the night he'd snapped awake suddenly with his mind whirling and dread creeping up on him once more. Bliss must have had her copies too. Copies of his credit card charges to her 1-900 phone sex line. Lattrell forced himself to calm down and think rationally. Right now most people in the industry were thinking that he'd been locked in a room with a mystery man. But Phe-Nom had also put it out there that Lattrell might have been on the phone with a dude named Reggie.

It was a real long shot, and nobody in the world

would probably put two and two together, but stranger things had been known to happen when money and careers were at stake. If by chance the planets lined up and Phe-Nom was able to prove that Lattrell was talking on a sex line at the same time he was banging on his door, there would be no stopping the rumor train. He would never be able to prove it was really a woman on the line, and the original accusation would always stand stronger than anything he might offer in defense.

Lattrell sat up the rest of the night thinking. By the time dawn broke, he had come up with a sketchy plan. He had sent Bliss a few CDs and other promo items from time to time. She'd given him a P.O. box address in Brooklyn, and he knew she'd received everything because her and Neck had both thanked him kindly.

He had to make a plea to Bliss. He needed to talk to her, and not on a sex line but face-to-face, heart-to-heart. Lattrell needed to get his credit card records from her and personally destroy them. That was the only way he'd ever feel completely safe, feel like all of his tracks had been wiped clean.

He clicked open his cell phone and dialed. "Hey," Lattrell said when his boy Twenty answered. "We need to make a run to New York in a few days. Yeah. I'll let you know when. Just wait for my call."

CHAPTER 11

THE sun was settling low on the horizon as Gary Browning held his beautiful wife of thirty years in his arms and watched her take her last breath.

"Lovin' Felicia . . ." Gary crooned in a voice that cracked with grief, "is easy 'cause she's wonderful . . ."

The staff at Family Hospice had left the room to give the couple privacy in their final minutes together, and Gary had spent that time telling Felicia all the things he'd been telling her for the past thirty years.

No matter how prepared Gary thought he was for her death, the end had rushed up on him with a suddenness that nearly robbed him of the foundation on which he stood. Felicia's body was pliant in his arms and she looked beautiful in her earth-toned silk smock. Her hair was a bit tousled on one side and her mouth had gone slack, but Gary bent his head and kissed her lips deeply, savoring the essence of her one last time.

He held her for the longest while. There had been only the two of them and now he was virtually alone in the world. He had never blamed Felicia for being infertile, but for the first time he wished that they'd had a child together. Someone who would have been an extension of his wife left on this earth to comfort him.

Felicia, in her wise and practical way, had made all of her funeral arrangements and there was very little for Gary to do. In the days following her death a steady stream of friends and colleagues flowed through the house bearing food, cards, hugs, and tears. Everybody had warm, funny stories to tell about Felicia, and there was always an arm extended in love and support toward Gary. He managed to get through the days reasonably well, but the nights were cold and lonely. He slept on her side of the bed, grasping her pillow, soaking it with his tears.

The funeral was surreal. No amount of time or talking could have prepared Gary for the sight of his beautiful wife lying in a coffin. He'd broken down so badly that his friend Matthew Yarbridge had insisted that Gary come stay with him for a few days.

Gary had accepted the offer mainly because he was too weak to fight, but also because Matthew was someone who had lost his wife too and who completely understood Gary's pain. The two men stayed together in Matthew's penthouse suite for a week, sometimes talking, most times not. They ate when they were hungry, slept when they were tired. They were there for each other and they left each other alone.

At the end of the week Gary went home. It felt strange walking into the house he had shared with Felicia. Even though she had been in hospice care for many months, her spirit had still been alive in the house. But as Gary moved through the rooms that had once been filled with the essence of his wife, the full realization hit him that she would never again dwell there.

Picking through the mail, Gary was both frightened and exhilarated to find a letter addressed to him and bearing his wife's handwriting. He sat down at the kitchen table and tore into it with shaking fingers and began to read.

Moments later he was bewildered. Hearing Felicia's words from the grave was a great comfort, but what she was asking him to do was far too much, too soon.

Trust me, baby. I know it seems hard. But you have to do this. Do it for me, for yourself. For us.

Gary was torn. How could she think him capable of such a thing? Why would she ask something so cruel and unreasonable of him? Didn't she know he'd be weak right now? Didn't she know he'd be much too vulnerable?

Staggering into their bedroom, Gary collapsed on the bed. He wailed out loud, like a newborn baby, thrashing about and screaming as his eyes traveled over every item in the room, every item that was the embodiment of Felicia.

What seemed like hours later he had cried himself dry. He lay there hiccupping and moaning, clutching the bedspread in his fists. He'd expended a lot of energy trying to run from the task his wife had set for him, but it was still there, hanging heavy on his heart.

It took him all day and most of the night, but he did it. Box after box, memory after memory, Gary savored each item briefly, then packed it all away. By the time the sun rose the next morning there was a stack of boxes in the driveway and nothing of Felicia left to be found in Gary's home. The memory of his wife lived safely in his heart, where he knew he was free to keep her forever.

He forced himself to eat a bowl of Cheerios, then take a shower. Exhaustion coursed through his body and his heart was wrung dry. Gary had made a lot of phone calls to notify friends and some of Felicia's distant family members of her passing, but there was one call that he hadn't made. One person that he hadn't told, someone who he felt really, really needed to know. Gary took off his robe and sat on the side of his bed. Swinging his legs into a comfortable position he picked up the phone and clicked the talk button. He hesitated for only a moment, then dialed 1-900-A-N-Y-T-I-M-E.

Joe Godfrey tore through his wife's walk-in closet in a rage.

He'd come in to put one of her purses on a shelf, and when he did several others toppled down to the floor. Joe was surprised as he picked up the multicolored array of pocketbooks and one fell open, its contents sliding to the carpet.

He fingered the stack of documents, curious why several months' worth of credit card receipts would be hidden in such a manner. Sitting down on the floor, Joe sorted the receipts by date and spread them out in front of him. Scrutinizing each debit, he noticed a recurring charge that was outside of the usual Internet fee, life insurance, and cell phone bill.

It was a 1-900 number, and Godfrey had seen enough late-night infomercials to know what type of services were offered under those plans. Prior to marrying Sally he'd called a few of them himself but always found the person on the line to sound artificial and bored, and no matter how sexy she sounded, Joe could never stop himself from visualizing her as someone who looked like his grandmother.

There seemed to be a pattern to the charges, with the calls occurring roughly once a week over a period of several months. Joe knew lots of men who got their jollies off by having phone sex with an anonymous woman, but why on earth would his wife be calling such a number? And if there was some sort of benign explanation behind it all, why hide the credit card bills in the bottom of an old purse?

An old familiar rage rose up in Joe's gut that no amount of reasonable self-talk could quell. Sally knew how he felt about cheaters. About liars. He'd been deceived and humiliated in his first marriage and he'd sworn that no woman would ever get away with treating him so badly again.

Joe ripped the closet apart, dumping out every purse and running his fingers in the toe of every shoe. He turned her pockets inside out, felt along the brim of her winter hats, emptied out her dresser drawers, and shook out every item that his wife had neatly folded.

What he was looking for, he wasn't sure. But if he found it somebody was going to have hell to pay. Joe stormed from the closet, taking the old bills with him. He snatched a phone from a dresser and tried Sally's cell, then cursed and threw the phone on the bed when the call went straight to her voice mail. She was at a day conference and couldn't be reached until 6:00 PM. Joe sat down on their bed with a growing sense of anger and dread coursing through his veins. This better not be what he thought it was. It just better not. He picked up the phone again, then dialed the number that had incurred the charges on his credit card bill. It was 1-900-A-N-Y-T-I-M-E.

It wasn't unusual for the phone to ring in the Purple Room when there was no client on Bliss's schedule, but it was pretty unusual for certain clients to call outside of their normal times.

Especially this one.

Bliss sat with her hand hovering above the telephone as the caller ID flashed with a name and number that for the past year had been regular down to the second. Not only wasn't it this particular client's day to call, this wasn't her time slot, and Bliss was suspicious.

"Hello," she said, picking up on the fourth ring and making her voice sound neutral and cheery.

"Er, hello." It was a man. A white man. "Whom might I ask am I speaking to?"

Alarm bells went off in Bliss's head and she kept her tone light and upbeat, as though she was a young white woman.

"Whom might I ask are you trying to reach?"

"Er . . . I'm not really sure. My, um, someone has been calling this number and charging the call to my credit card. I'm just trying to find out who might be calling and what they might be needing a sex line for."

Bliss thought fast. There was no need to pretend she wasn't a pay-for-call service, but she wasn't about to give up any information on her client, either.

"Well, I have a confidentiality agreement with all of my clients. However, if there have been unauthorized charges to your credit card then I can certainly understand why you'd be concerned. Is there anyone besides you who has access to your credit card?"

"Er, yes. My wife. My wife has access to this card."

"Can you tell me her name, sir?"

"Her name is Sally. Sally Godfrey."

Bliss threw her head back and laughed.

"*Sally!* Oh, Sally-Sally! My attorney, Sally! You must

be Mr. Godfrey, Sally's husband! So good to meet you! This is funny! Your wife is one of the attorneys who are working on my case. And so far she seems to be a damn fine attorney at that. I'm disabled, you know. It's a long story that begins with Gulf War syndrome and ends with someone who looks like me, but anywho, your wife is helping with my legal brief and since this is the only line I have, she's used it quite a bit to call me. Oh my God! This is so funny! Wait till I tell her! You thought she was calling a phone sex line!"

There was uneasy laughter from the man, and then a deep sigh of relief. "Whew! Well you certainly don't have to tell her unless you want to! Actually, I'm pretty embarrassed. Ashamed of myself too. My insecurities and imagination ran amok because for a minute I was actually worried that my wife might be cheating on me!"

Bliss laughed again, her voice silky smooth. "I haven't actually met your wife in person, Mr. Godfrey—"

"Please, call me Joe."

"Right, Joe. I haven't actually met your wife in person but we talk on the phone so regularly that I feel as though I know her. You can relax, I'm sure. Sally just doesn't seem like the cheating type. She brags about you all the time and she always sounds so happy."

"But I don't understand . . . if you're just a client, why'd she hide the bills? That doesn't make sense . . ."

Bliss's tone went low. "Maybe she hid them because she didn't want you to know . . . she didn't want you to know that I'm not paying her."

"What?"

"I'm not paying her. I'm disabled and I can't afford to. Your wife is representing me pro bono, from the goodness of her heart. Sometimes people don't like to broadcast their good works. They just want to do them."

"I hadn't thought of that," Joe said slowly. "It makes sense, though. Sally is so kind. So loving. She's always going out on a limb for someone. I'm not surprised that she would want to help you for free. I don't think she needed to hide it, but I'm not surprised that she decided to do it."

Bliss brightened. "Great! I'm just happy you called to get the facts for yourself. Most men would have gone off the deep end with the accusations and finger-pointing before checking things out."

"Well, to be honest Sally is at a conference today and I can't reach her. I probably would have responded like most men if I'd had the opportunity. In fact, I just anni-hilated her clothes closet and dumped everything out of her dresser drawers. I guess I'd better go clean up before she gets home and wonders if I've gone crazy."

Bliss giggled. "Yes, you should probably get that cleaned up. Look, Joe, I know how it is . . . how about we keep this little conversation just between us, huh? I know it's not healthy for husbands and wives to keep secrets from each other, but I don't think it'll hurt this one time, do you?"

Bliss hung up thinking that she'd handled that situation well, if she had to say so herself. And the following Monday morning when Sally Godfrey made her usual call, instead of pretending to be a redheaded biker chick wearing leather chaps and no drawers, Bliss informed her that one Mr. Joe Godfrey had found her stash of credit card bills and called to find out exactly who was fucking his wife.

"Oh my God," Sally had said, her voice panic filled and breathless. "Please. You didn't say anything, did you? What did you tell him?"

"Oh, we had quite the chat." Bliss had laughed, then quickly reassured her worried client. "And by the time we finished your husband was convinced that you're madly in love with him and embarrassed that he'd made himself look like such an ass."

"What did you say?"

"Since there was no need pretending this wasn't a sex line, I told him that I was your client. I said you were representing me in a case that I was bringing against the federal government for wrongful exposure to toxic chemicals."

"What?!?"

"My father had Gulf War syndrome and he died from multiple cancers and other chemical-related diseases. But not before producing a physically deformed child. Me."

There was stark silence on the other end of the line, and Bliss realized that she'd completely blown Sally's fantasy and had probably lost her forever as a client.

"You told my husband that?"

"Yes, I did."

Sally exhaled a long sigh of relief.

"Thank God. Thank *you*. You've saved my marriage, Bliss. And probably my life. I don't know what I'd do if he ever found out the truth . . . Thank you, Bliss. Thank you. How can I repay you?"

Bliss thought briefly. Sally might not be her client anymore, but that didn't mean she couldn't be Sally's.

"Well, I told him you were representing me for free. So how about you just do what I already said you were doing."

"Huh?"

"Become my lawyer, Sally," Bliss said. "Represent my case. For free."

"But that's not my specialty area, Bliss. I'm not a personal injury lawyer. I work with sexual deviants."

Bliss laughed. "Then stretch yourself. That's what I do when I'm with you. Explore a new area of the law. And by the way," she added, knowing that she could definitely cross Sally off as a client after this, "you can call me Bertha from now on. Bertha Sampson."

CHAPTER 12

WNEW-TV was located in the Purity Plaza, a twelve-story building in midtown Manhattan that boasted two doormen, a Starbucks, and several small specialty shops. The telethon had been widely advertised, and the Yarbridge Foundation had sent a limousine to Bertha's apartment at 8:00 AM sharp. The day had come too quickly, and no matter how much Bertha loved Matthew Yarbridge, she wished like hell she could crawl under her bed and hide for the rest of the century. When Hyacinth came in to help her get dressed Bertha had played sick and tried to beg off, but Hyacinth wasn't having it and forty-five minutes later she was wheeling Bertha into a large, comfortable reception area where a television staff awaited her.

They were greeted warmly by a slender white woman with a big, pretty smile.

"Hi, I'm Rita," she said, smiling briefly at Bertha and then extending her hand to Hyacinth.

Rita had a beach body beneath the pale pink swing dress she was wearing and her sleek blond hair hung around her shoulders in perfect layers. Bertha took a quick glance at the gorgeous young thing, then looked down in her lap and fiddled with her old paisley cotton scarf. The sexy white woman was the exact physical image that Bertha sold to most of her clients in their fantasies, and having the real thing so close in the flesh was unsettling.

"They're expecting you in the makeup room," Rita told Hyacinth. "When you're done, Mr. Yarbridge will meet you in the studio."

Bertha kept her head down as Rita gave Hyacinth directions to the makeup room. She noticed how the young lady directed her conversation to Hyacinth, even though it was Bertha who would be appearing on camera.

Nothing had changed in the world of the able-bodied, Bertha could tell, wishing she had stayed her ass at home. People were still ignorant as hell. They took one look at her body and her wheelchair and decided she was either inept or incapacitated. Sure, the countless surgeries had done wonders for her physical appearance and these days people didn't run and curse when they saw her. Bertha's own mirror told her she looked normal enough not to scare folks away. But she was still disfigured. There was no hiding that. And in most people's minds, a physical disfigurement meant an automatic mental or intellectual disability, and that's why Bertha didn't like it out here. She preferred to stay in her home with her computer and her telephone and leave the outside world to those on the outside.

Hyacinth paused outside a doorway and tapped Bertha on the shoulder.

"Hang in there. Everything is going to be fine, okay?"

Bertha didn't answer. She should have stayed her ass at home.

The makeup room was stuffy and the lead guy was nervous about applying chemicals to Bertha's skin.

"Her skin looks so . . . so . . . *sensitive*," he commented to Hyacinth over Bertha's head. Bertha glanced up and busted him frowning and holding his powder brush away like he was scared to use it on her. "I'm not sure it's a good idea to even put makeup on her if she has some sort of chronic skin condition."

Bertha sighed and just sat there as he stared at his tiny bag of studio makeup like it was fit for Oprah. His ignorant ass wasn't talking to her, and he sure didn't give a damn about her opinion. She almost laughed thinking about the stockpile of glamour makeup she worked with every day. She might have bad skin, but she had damned good taste. She ordered the best skin products off the Internet that money could buy, and what she had stashed in the Purple Room made his funky-ass little travel kit look like kindergarten shit.

After a bunch of hemming and hawing, he broke out a disposable applicator and powdered just her shine spots, and minutes later Bertha was being wheeled into the studio where Matthew Yarbridge and several co-hosts were going through last-minute preparations on the telethon set.

Bertha watched a lot of television but she'd never imagined herself in a studio environment. She eyed Matthew as he conducted himself before the camera with ease. There was such power in his presence. He was physically fit and he looked so virile and strong. His movements were assured, his voice, his demeanor, all exuded confidence and a sensuality that gave Bertha a sexual rush that was stunning in its intensity.

She stared at his broad back, mesmerized as she built

a fantasy around him. His navy pin-striped suit and baby blue shirt appeared crisp on the director's camera and his salt-and-pepper hair made him look experienced and trustworthy.

"Would you like some bottled water?" A young producer tapped Bertha's arm, interrupting her thoughts as she actually spoke to her. She was a sweet-faced Hispanic girl pulling a cart of juice, water, and assorted snacks.

"We also have tea and coffee, if you'd prefer something hot," the girl offered, and Bertha thanked her and declined, although she was grateful that somebody was finally speaking to her like she actually existed.

The telethon was being broadcast around the country and Bertha was scheduled to kick it off by singing the national anthem. Matthew came over as they were readying the set for her. Bertha watched him stride toward her with a big grin on her face. She accepted his outstretched hand and rose from her wheelchair and practically threw herself in his arms.

"You look gorgeous," he said, giving her a big fatherly hug.

Bertha held on to him, deeply inhaling his cologne. She was in heaven. She'd missed Matthew. Coming out this morning was more about being close to him than it was about raising money. There wasn't much she wouldn't do to get next to him, and even though he was old enough to be her father, Bertha had always known they shared something special between them.

"Hi, Matthew," Bertha purred shyly when she finally let him go. She knew the seductive power of her voice, and she knew how to use it. "You're looking wonderful too."

"Thanks for agreeing to help the foundation. I know how resistant you are to the outside world, Bertha, but I think it can be good for you to mingle with real people occasionally, you know."

"Oh, Matthew!"

Bertha felt herself slipping. Slipping straight into Bliss.

She threw her head back and her eyes tinkled. Her voice was sweeter than caramelized peaches as she put her hand on his arm and grinned sexily. "You know you don't have to thank me. Mingling with you is my greatest pleasure. I just wish we could mingle much more often. And in many more ways."

Matthew hugged her again. He kissed a spot above the corner of her lip.

"You've always been so sweet, Bertha. I've missed you. We'll have dinner soon, okay?"

Bertha turned up the heat. "Don't keep me waiting too long, Matthew," she practically moaned, her voice sounding like a mini orgasm. "Let's make it really, really soon."

Matthew didn't respond. Instead he patted her arm, then unhooked her walker from the back of her wheel-chair and helped her toward her designated area of the set. He introduced her to his co-hostess, Sylena Scott, and a few studio technicians, and minutes later Bertha was ready to begin.

Standing under the bright lights, Bertha closed her eyes momentarily. She thought about all those years of being wheeled down a hushed church aisle. Huddled beneath her yellow blanket, Little Bertha could taste the anticipation in the air, and it was awful knowing that when that cover was finally yanked off everyone in the room was going to run away horrified by what they saw.

A lot of that same fear was in her now. That bubbly, sick feeling in the pit of her stomach that said her ugliness was about to be exposed to the world. Once again Bertha's blanket was about to be snatched away, and although she'd come a long way from the days of causing folks to flee from the sideshow freak, she comforted herself with the knowledge that she still had what it took to bring the masses back.

Bertha Sampson could still sang, baby. She could *sang*.

Cho Lee Yung smelled the rat the moment he opened the door. Waving his hand in front of his nose, he locked the door behind him and clicked on the overhead lights, then pressed the remote control and turned on the morning news.

It was warm inside the restaurant and the air was stagnant as he walked around checking his traps. He struck gold after looking behind a bin of molding potatoes, and the offending rat carcass was already swollen and smelly as he freed it from the trap and flushed it down the toilet, returning it to the city sewers where it had probably come from.

It was payday in the world of welfare, and soon the recipients of public assistance would be using their benefits to purchase groceries and other items from the local stores and eateries. Spending moods were always high on check days, and Cho anticipated stacking some of that money in his cash register. There was a time when he'd accepted food stamps for egg rolls, then passed them off to a friend downtown who converted them at a premium, but those days were long in the past.

Recipients had debit cards these days, which made it a lot harder to bypass the system.

Cho set about the business of his day, chopping vegetables and soaking rice to be steamed and fried. He checked his trays of leftover meats and determined they were all fragrant but passable for at least another day. His delivery boy came in at eight thirty, and Cho sent him out back to bag trash and hose down the food compactor.

At 9:00 AM the chimes jingled on his front door and a young black girl pushing a double stroller struggled her way inside. She rolled two boys, an infant and a toddler, toward the counter and glanced up at the menu board.

"Umm." She strummed her grimy six-inch nails on the counter and squinted. "Let me get a half order of ribs, an order of fries, and four chicken wings."

The girl had crayon-colored braids in her hair and the children were coughing and dirty. Cho scribbled his nonsense on the small white pad, adding nearly a dollar fifty to the correct total. Cho watched, wide-eyed as the toddler spit his swollen pacifier out on the floor, and the young mother calmly picked it up, sucked it for a few seconds, then placed it back in the baby's mouth.

"You got any milk?" she asked.

Cho shook his head. "No, sowwy," he said in his fake

accent. He didn't carry milk in his restaurant, but for the first time ever he wished he did.

"Wait!" he said, passing his commercial storage unit and heading in the back toward his small personal refrigerator. He came back holding out a small bottle, grinning.

"Apple juice," Cho said, nodding toward the children. "You no pay. For the baby."

The girl accepted the juice and stuck it in a bag that hung from the back of the stroller.

"Eight fifty," Cho said, circling the total on the sheet and holding out his hand.

The girl glanced at the menu again, then narrowed her eyes and glared at him.

"How you figure?"

"Pardon me?" Cho was taken aback. He had never been challenged before.

"How you come up with eight fifty, mister?"

"You want half order ribs, riiiigh?" Cho ticked off on his fingers. "French fry and four chick wing. That eight fifty." He stared at the young black girl with conviction in his eyes.

She stared at him right back.

"*Noooo*," she said, holding her head to the side defiantly. "It says right there on your menu that a half order of ribs is four dollars and your wing and fry special is two fifty. That comes out to six fifty."

"Plus tax."

"Tax is 8.375% in Brooklyn, mister. My bill comes out to seven dollars and four cents. So where you get some eight fifty? Where'd the other dollar forty-six come from?"

Cho swallowed hard. "Apple juice?"

The girl reached inside her bag and flung the bottle of apple juice over the counter. It struck the brick wall above the stove and shattered, sending liquid and glass spraying everywhere.

"You fuckin' cheat!" she screamed, wheeling her babies toward the door and cursing Cho out the whole way. "Y'all think all black people are fuckin *stupid*! Some of us can *count*, motherfucker! Come up in our goddamn neighborhoods trying to take advantage of us all the time like we ignorant! I should call the cops on your thieving ass!"

Cho was trembling as the young girl stormed outside with her children, screaming obscenities at him as she accused people like him of being the main reason that blacks were so disrespected and oppressed in their own neighborhoods. Several people on the street stopped to stare as she pointed toward the restaurant and raged, and Cho saw many of them nodding their heads as though they agreed with her.

Stunned didn't describe what Cho was feeling. There had been nothing about the girl's appearance to even remotely suggest she was any smarter than the rest of his customers. Yet this young mother of two had challenged Cho's thinking in a way that surprised him. Not only didn't she back down from his assertion, she'd stood up for her own and had outthought him in a situation where Cho had always had the upper hand. Cho was embarrassed and his cheeks were red as he cleaned up the broken glass and sticky juice. Not because he'd padded the girl's bill, but because he'd been caught. He may not have been Chinese, but he *was* Asian, and the illusion of honor still held importance in his life.

Grateful that his young delivery boy had not been on hand to witness his shaming, Cho finished cleaning and poured a capful of sesame oil in a hot pan and began cooking the vegetables that he'd cut up earlier. His cheeks were red, both from the black girl's chiding and from the rising steam as he listened to the newscaster on WNEW-TV reporting on a telethon that was being held to benefit the physically disfigured and disabled.

Cho's ears perked up as he listened to the broadcast. He thought about his mother and the horrible physical disfigurements she'd suffered. It still broke his heart to remember how people who didn't understand her beauty often looked at her with horror and disgust. He'd never heard of the foundation that the telethon was benefiting, but he hoped they'd raise enough money to meet their goals.

His delivery boy had completed his tasks and was now manning the counter while Cho cooked. Using a large potholder, Cho turned off the industrial burner and lifted the sizzling pan from the stove. He was just transferring the hot contents to a metal storage dish when a sound so beautiful, so piercing, so virginal, and *so familiar* blared from his television speaker that the hot pan went crashing to the floor as his arms flew into the air.

It was her. It was *her!*

He glared at the screen, his eyes wide, his jaw slack.

She was black! My God! She was *black!*

But . . . Cho realized as he gazed at her tight, scarred face and her broken, perversely shaped body . . . she was also beautiful.

Juicy Wings of Seattle was a popular gathering spot for sports enthusiasts and those who worked for one of the four technology giants nearby. Known for the killer wing sauce recipe concocted by the owner's wife, there was usually a long waiting list during lunchtime, which Jim Burgess preferred to avoid.

Jim was in town for a business meeting and had been tasked to arrange a lunchtime pitch for one of Microsoft's newest software programs to several overseas reps. Treating them to a feast of Juicy Wings and coleslaw was his idea of an American treat. He'd gone into the local office briefly, then left at 8:30 and was sitting at the bar in Juicy Wings at 9:00 AM sharp.

If Jim thought he'd be the only businessman in Seattle who wanted to cater Juicy Wings for a Monday lunch, he was sorely mistaken. There were five other people waiting ahead of him at the customer service desk, and Jim joined them for a complimentary breakfast of hot wings, cheese, and fresh fruit as the morning news blared on one of the four large wall-mounted screens.

"These suckers are da bomb," a black young woman sitting beside Jim said as she turned to give him a sloppy-sauced grin.

Jim cringed. Sauce covered her fingers and she'd gnawed a wing down to the bone and was working on the gristle.

With an unmistakable look of disgust on his face, Jim

turned slightly on his stool, giving the young woman his shoulder. With her tacky braids, endless rolls of arm fat, and garishly huge lips, she represented everything that Jim detested.

Thumbing through the catering brochure, Jim bit into a wing and tried to decide between the deluxe package that fed "up to twenty-five" and the grand-slam package that cost twice as much but fed "up to forty" and included extras like broccoli, cauliflower, carrot sticks, and celery.

A squirt of wing sauce dripped from his fingers, narrowly missing his lapel. Jim grabbed a napkin from the counter and tucked it into his collar like a bib, then adjusted his glasses and dug back into his pile of wings in earnest. He was just running over the menu items again when the opening words of the national anthem were emitted from the television set. Jim froze with a dripping wing halfway between his plate and his mouth.

He *knew* her.

He looked up at the screen and every hair on his neck stood rigid. A sweet melody filled the air, and all eyes in the room were pulled toward the mounted plasma screen on the wall.

The woman on the screen was the stuff of Jim's nightmares.

The voice coming out of her mouth had stroked him in his most intimate dreams, but the girl standing there was a hideous reminder of his tortured past.

Jim's shirt went tight at the collar and his scalp broke out in a sweat. He closed his eyes briefly, then forced himself to open them again. Her voice was like a harp. Sweet and angelic. Jim forced himself to look at the screen again, and when he did his skin began to crawl in disgust.

She was *black*.

Hooker black. Nasty black. The physical embodiment of his filthy disease.

Rage nearly suffocated him and the cloistering scent of cheap perfume burned his nose. His groin swelled and his bowels pressed. He could actually feel the disgusting virus swirling around in his blood. Jim wiped his mouth with the back of his hand. His breath hitched as a piece of chicken lodged in his throat.

"Are you okay?" A cute young lady sitting beside him asked. She was an advertising executive hoping to impress a big firm over lunch. She'd been sneaking glances at Jim ever since he'd come through the door and thought he was one of the most handsome, virile-looking men she'd ever seen. She put her hand on his muscular shoulder. "Can I get you a glass of water?"

Jim shook her off. The half-eaten chicken wing slid down his lap and fell to the floor, along with the catering menu. Struggling to his feet, Jim leaned on the table briefly, then tore the napkin from his throat and flung it aside.

Bliss sang so beautifully. Her voice evoked images of a strawberry blonde with a long white, virginal dress. Someone clean and pure. A runner who ate properly, drank lots of water, and guarded her chastity.

Pressing his hands over his ears, Jim Burgess staggered from the table and burst through the restaurant doors, grateful for the honking horns and blessed chaotic sounds of the noisy city streets outside.

CHAPTER 13

GARY had overslept by an hour, something he hadn't done in over a quarter of a century. He awakened to unfamiliar surroundings, his bedroom stark and picked clean. He moved slowly toward the bathroom, remembering the framed prints that had once been on the walls, the odd knickknacks that had covered the shelves. Even the bathroom was different. No more frilly, hand-sewn towel holders and "for show" items that he'd never been allowed to touch.

Raking his fingers through his thinning hair, Gary entered the shower and stood under a spray of steaming water and willed it to clear his mind. He had important business to attend to this morning. His friend Matthew was depending on him, and there was no way he could let him down.

Thirty minutes later he'd downed a weak cup of coffee and was sitting in the backseat of a taxicab. It would take him about fifteen minutes to reach the studio, but traffic was no heavier than normal and he should get there right on time.

Gary sat back and scanned the city streets through the eyes of a lonely man. It had been a couple of weeks since Felicia's funeral and he'd received several letters from her since that date. He had no idea which friend she'd entrusted to mail them, nor did he care to know. He counted her words from the grave as a blessing and a mercy, and he was grateful that she had been wise enough to foresee his grief and his need.

It still puzzled him, this request of Felicia's that he give away those of her things that meant the most to him. Her letter had been very specific and she'd been adamant that this was something that Gary must accomplish, and while it bewildered him to no end, Gary trusted his wife's judgment. Then and now, he trusted *her*.

The taxi arrived at the Purity Plaza at 8:55 AM and Gary paid the driver and tipped him kindly. He rode a crowded elevator up to the twelfth floor and was ushered into the studio by a pleasant young woman with long blond hair.

"You're right on time!" she said with a grin after Gary introduced himself. "Mr. Yarbridge just sent a message that he's expecting you. We went live less than a minute ago and already the phone lines are lighting up. Come on back. They've got a special guest onstage who's about to sing the national anthem, and from what I've been told, this is something we won't want to miss."

Gary followed the young lady back to the set where the singing of the national anthem had just begun, and the sound struck him even before the dark curtains were parted. It was serene, it was a balm of comfort. It was a plea from the soul, a lullaby that promised rest for the weary. It was a tranquil hand that stilled his heart, it was a welcome respite from grief and pain. It was love and it was *lovin'*. It was his wife in the spirit.

It was Bliss.

"Whoa," Rita said, gripping the older man under his arm. "You feeling okay?" Gary had staggered against her, nearly knocking her down, and her first thought was that he'd been stricken ill.

"Is everything all right? Do you need to sit down?"

Gary leaned on the receptionist transfixed, gazing in wonderment at the woman who stood singing into the microphone. Finally, after long moments, he looked at Rita, then down at his feet. "Cable." He swallowed hard and nodded toward the ground. He shrugged and righted himself. "I must have tripped on a cable."

"Oh," Rita said doubtfully. She held on to him a few seconds longer, then smiled as he straightened his jacket and tie.

"She's got some voice, huh?" he said, almost to himself.

"Absolutely." Rita nodded. "I don't think I've ever heard anything like it before. She gave me goose bumps."

"Just stunning. Tell me, what is her name again?"

Rita looked at the schedule on her clipboard. "Bertha. That's Bertha Sampson."

"Bertha," Gary said softly. His lips seemed to caress each consonant. He turned to face Rita. "I have a package I'd like to send Ms. Sampson. It's a gift from my corporation for her appearance on our telethon. Would you happen to have her mailing address on file?"

Rita nodded. "Certainly, sir. I can email it to your secretary, or I can write it down for you at the end of this segment if you like."

"Actually . . ." Gary began. He forced himself to tear his eyes off Bliss as he turned toward the pretty white woman and smiled. He held out his arm and she took it and allowed herself to be led away. "I'd like to get that address now, if you don't mind."

"Bertha, that was incredible," Matthew said as he led her toward the reception area. His eyes were gleaming and Bertha had never seen him so excited.

"The call center was ablaze during your entire segment. From the moment you sang the national anthem until you stepped off the stage, there wasn't a break in the incoming calls, and I can only imagine what your segment's pledges will amount to."

Bertha nodded and held on to his rock-hard arm as Hyacinth walked beside them pushing the wheelchair. She knew Matthew was walking very slowly on her account and although she could have moved a little faster, she milked it for all it was worth.

"I'm just happy that I was able to help, Matthew. After everything the foundation has done for me"—she stole a sly glance at Hyacinth as she parroted the older woman's words—"this was my opportunity to give back in some small way. I truly understand that someone has to sacrifice in order for me to live the kind of life that I live. As a disabled person I depend on the kindness and generosity of people like you and Hyacinth for my medical care and my daily living. How selfish would I be if I was too good to get on television and encourage others to help? What kind of woman would I be?"

Matthew nodded his agreement and graced her with a broad smile. "You're the kind of woman who has a lot to offer the entire world, Bertha. The kind of beautiful girl who makes an old man like me proud. It was heartening to hear you stand before the nation and tell your story with so much honesty and compassion. I can remember the first time I saw you being wheeled down the aisle of that church like it was yesterday. I knew right away that there was some sort of scam going on at your expense. I think it's high time the whole world knows how often the disabled are used and preyed upon by the wicked and the greedy. Telling the world your life story today was a big step for you, I'm aware of that. But to whom much is given, much is required. It's an even bigger step for the disabled community that you represent."

Bertha smiled at him and sighed. She'd had no intention of going on television and telling all her business, but after the rousing applause they'd given her for singing the national anthem, and the way Sylena Scott had sat next to Bertha and kissed her hands, and told her how beautiful and brave she was, Bertha had felt herself getting teary-eyed and letting it all hang out.

"Well, you can certainly pay me back. Remember," she told Matthew. They were approaching the bank of elevators and Hyacinth was indicating that Bertha should get in her chair, "you promised to have dinner with me."

Matthew grinned. "Okay, Bertha. You're right. I promised. We'll do dinner. You can decide when and where."

Bertha giggled. "Tomorrow evening. My apartment."

He looked surprised. "Wouldn't you rather go out? A five-star restaurant with an elegant wait staff?"

Hell no! was Bertha's first thought. She was trying to get Matthew's fine ass in the Purple Room so she could jump his bones! But instead she said, "No thanks. After spending an hour on live television running my mouth I think I've had enough of the outside world to last me a good long while. We can order in something at my place. I've got the latest music and a few great movies too. My place." She giggled again. "Tomorrow. Five o'clock. Don't be late."

Bertha was still smiling as Matthew helped her into her wheelchair and Hyacinth backed her into the elevator car. She winked at Matthew and waved, and as she waited for the doors to close a handsome middle-aged black man walked up to Matthew and, with his eyes on Bertha, touched Matthew's shoulder and the two men shook hands warmly.

The man was a bit shorter than Matthew but very handsome and fit. Bertha had no idea who he was, but his eyes held the most beautiful sadness she'd ever seen and he seemed to be staring at her with more than a little intensity.

"Who's that?" Bertha asked Hyacinth, pulling her scarf around her shoulders as the elevator doors slid closed and both men disappeared from sight.

"That's Gary Browning," Hyacinth answered with reverence ringing in her voice. "He's Matthew's dear friend and one of the most powerful men in town."

Jim Burgess suffered through his Monday meetings, stumbling badly on portions of his proposals that he usually sailed through like a pro. It was late when he returned to his hotel, and after packing his bags he caught a taxi to the airport where he had a two-hour wait for the red-eye flight that would take him back to New York.

His body moved on autopilot and it was all he could

do to keep his rage contained. A chatty young lady stepped on the back of Jim's foot while moving through the security line and his first instinct was to drop his bags and dig his fingers into her throat. A couple ahead of him, barely out of their teens, infuriated him with their public promiscuity. The man had spiked hair dyed orange and multiple facial piercings that should have set off the security alarms, and the girl wore a skirt that was so short that Jim thought he could see her pubic hair. The two sat in the waiting area kissing and fondling each other without the slightest embarrassment, and Jim had to force himself to stand and walk away when what he really wanted to do was backhand the girl across her filthy mouth and toss her boyfriend out onto the rain-soaked tarmac.

He spent the five-hour flight seething in anger, betrayal, and humiliation. The smell of cheap perfume seemed to come at him from every direction. Despite being awake for nearly twenty-four hours, Jim never closed his eyes during the entire flight. He arrived home before dawn on Tuesday morning and spent two hours typing mandatory reports then uploading them to a Microsoft database.

With his company work done, Jim got personal. He scanned his email account until he found what he was looking for. What a liar. There was no way the monstrosity he'd seen on television could have been eating properly or performing any of the exercises he'd been sending her. Bliss. Bertha Sampson. Bliss. The thought of what he'd been making love to sickened Jim, and he rushed into the bathroom and threw up in the sink.

Back at his computer he logged on to a secure search program and entered an IP address. She would be easy to find. In a matter of moments a map flashed on his screen. A few keystrokes later Jim had accessed an online Yellow Page listing. He typed in "Bertha Sampson." A long list of addresses popped up. He cross-referenced them with the one he'd gotten from her Internet protocol and got a match: 67 Third Avenue, Brooklyn. Jim scribbled the address on a slip of paper. There was no need to consult MapQuest. He knew the area well.

On the brink of exhaustion, but with a deadly plan cemented in his mind, Jim crawled over to his bed and fell into a furious sleep. He spent the next ten hours dreaming blessed dreams of revenge.

CHAPTER 14

TWENTY waited outside the post office in downtown Brooklyn just like La-Rule had ordered him to. He was dressed in a starched shirt and tie and had a backpack slung over his shoulder. Twenty had gotten there ten minutes before opening and leaned on a car until he saw a postal employee unlock the front doors and retreat back to the counter.

Just twenty-four hours earlier, Twenty had mailed an envelope containing La-Rule's latest CD from this very same post office. It had been addressed to a P.O. box right in the lobby, and Twenty was on a mission to make sure he was on location with his eyes on target when the package was retrieved by the box owner.

"Excuse me." He approached the young Asian employee at the counter. "Can you tell me what time mail is delivered to the post office boxes?"

"Twelve o'clock," the short-haired lady said without looking up.

Twenty sauntered back outside to wait. La-Rule had told him not to take his eyes off that P.O. box until somebody showed up to pick up the mail, and that's exactly what he was gonna do. He leaned against a car and prepared himself to chill. He was ready to stand out there all day if he had to, because La-Rule was the money man who lined Twenty's pockets, and if the boss man said wait, then wait was Twenty's middle name.

Six and a half hours later Twenty was still in the same spot. He hadn't eaten, pissed, or barely blinked. In fact, he had been staring into the post office for so long that he had gone into a zone and had almost missed the tall, light-skinned old lady when she walked over to the boxes and stood smack in the area that Twenty was watching.

He'd bolted up the stairs and pulled open the doors before she was finished rolling the combination lock. Twenty had scoped out the area so thoroughly that he was certain she was fiddling with his box, and he slunk backward, out of her range, and waited until she pulled the bright blue envelope from the box that Twenty had addressed to "OCCUPANT" and mailed the day before.

"Yeah," Twenty muttered under his breath. "That's my baby."

He waited until the old lady had exited the post office, then followed her down the street, noting her walking pace but careful to stay back a good distance. She led him to an apartment building on a nice stretch of Third Avenue, and Twenty walked in like he was with her, then slipped into the elevator and smiled his best I'm-a-nice-young-student, smile.

The lady got off on the eighth floor, and Twenty stayed on the elevator, holding the door-open button as he noted which direction she walked down the hall. He counted her footsteps until he heard them stop, then grinned when a set of keys jangled, then turned in a lock.

Releasing the hold button, Twenty rode up one floor and got off. He turned in the same direction the old woman had turned, then did his best imitation of her walking pace and counted out the number of steps she had taken. At the end of his count there was only one apartment within range. It was on his left, apartment 9G.

"8G," Twenty said, searing Bliss's apartment into his memory. "The chick lives in 8G."

Bertha rocked the latest CD by rapper La-Rule as she got her act together for dinner. Her spirits had been sky-high since coming out of the studio the day before, and tonight she shuffled through her apartment chanting gangster rap with visions of dinner and hopefully a little dirty dancing with Matthew Yarbridge in her head.

"I can't believe I actually brought that trash home," Hyacinth said, shaking her head. "If I'd known what was in that envelope I would have thrown it away at the post office."

Bertha bopped her head to the beat. "I love La-Rule. He sticks his head in some of the funkiest places but underneath it all he's a decent guy. Besides, we all have our nasty little needs."

"I don't know what you're thinking," Hyacinth warned, "but you're acting a little frisky, Miss Thing. Matthew is only coming for dinner, remember? So don't go making no fool out of either one of you, okay?"

"What do you mean?" Bertha asked sarcastically. "Just because Matthew is physically able-bodied and I'm disabled, is that supposed to mean something?"

Hyacinth smirked. "No, Matthew is old and wise and you're young and dumb. *That's* supposed to mean something."

Bertha wasn't thinking about Hyacinth. Mother James might have found religion in her old age, but six children by five different men meant Hyacinth had a little freak in her too.

"I'm young, but I'm still grown," Bertha reminded her caregiver. "And if Matthew's not a fish then he won't bite. It's just that simple."

Hyacinth sighed and shook her head. She took her purse from a kitchen drawer and tucked it under her arm.

"Okay, hardhead. You don't know the first thing about men, Bertha. You stay cooped up in this house so much that you don't know enough about life, either. Enjoy your dinner tonight. Perhaps you'll wake up tomorrow not just one day older, but one day wiser."

Bertha sat staring at the door for long minutes after Hyacinth left. She loved that old lady like the mother she had never known, but there were a lot of things that Hyacinth didn't know about Bertha. She'd never been inside the Purple Room. She hadn't seen Bliss in action. If there was one thing in this world that Bertha knew, it was men. She knew what made them tick and what turned them on.

She knew how they thought and what they felt. Bertha aka Bliss was *every* woman, and Hyacinth didn't know a damn thing about what she could or couldn't do for Matthew. If Bliss couldn't get the man of her fantasies, then she had no business being the woman of anyone else's.

Bertha picked up the telephone and punched in the number she had memorized for Ming Su Yung's Chinese restaurant. When the telephone was answered she placed a special order for her favorite Chinese dish, then ordered an assortment of entrées and side items that she hoped Matthew would also enjoy.

When the telephone rang at 4:10 PM Cho Lee Yung was taking an order from an elderly customer and had four others waiting impatiently behind her in line. His afternoon worker was at the stove dunking wontons and chicken wings in overused vats of grease, and his delivery boy was rushing out the door holding a cut off box piled high with take-out orders.

"Scue me." Cho fake grinned at the tired-looking woman leaning on his counter as he picked up the phone. He was working frantically, unwilling to lose a customer on line at the expense of one on the phone, or vice versa.

"I was standing here before the phone rang, mister," the customer said. She had three children with her who were probably her grandkids, and Cho gave her a big smile and held up one finger. "Sowwy. Sowwy. Just one minute please, ma'am."

"Ming Su Yung's!" Cho sang into the telephone.

The very first word out the customer's mouth froze Cho in his tracks.

"Can I have a double order of beef and broccoli smothered in lobster sauce *and* peanut sauce? And can you add some sautéed shrimp to that and mix it all together real good?"

Even with a long line of hungry customers and an imbecile burning vegetables in his wok, Cho couldn't move.

"Hello? Did you hear me? *Hello*?"

Cho gasped. "You don't call on Tuesdays," he whispered, losing his accent and speaking in perfect English.

"I know." She giggled. "Hyacinth normally orders Chinese every Monday, but we were out yesterday so we missed. I'm making up for it tonight, though, and I'm even ordering a few extra dishes too."

Cho's hand shook so badly as he wrote down her order that he forgot to pad the bill. Waving his afternoon cook up to the front counter, Cho prepared the order himself, and when it was done he set everything in a cut off box and grabbed his hat.

"I'll be back," he told his cook, who glanced around the crowded restaurant, then looked at Cho with a bewildered glare. Customers were shifting from foot to foot, sighing impatiently as they waited to place their orders.

Cho waved off the man's questioning stare. "Answer the phones."

The jewelry box sat heavy in Gary's lap as he rode into Brooklyn by taxi. Twice already he'd knocked on the partition and started to ask the driver to turn around, but Felicia's wishes had been clear and more than anything Gary wanted to honor his wife.

Traffic was pretty heavy on the FDR Drive for a Tuesday, and Gary sat back and closed his eyes and tried hard to relax. He ran his hand over his face, feeling like he'd aged a hundred years in just one night.

Seeing Bliss at the telethon had thrown him.

He'd recognized her voice from the very first note of the national anthem, and there was no describing how shocked he'd been. In the back of his mind Gary had always known that he was calling a phone sex line. He'd never given a thought to what Bliss may have looked like or fantasized about her sexually. Gary's initial attraction to Bliss had come from her haunting, melodic voice that had so reminded him of his wife's. For him the thrill had always been emotional. The void she had filled in him had been in his heart.

That Bliss was disabled wasn't entirely shocking once Gary thought it through. He'd been around the block a time or two, and he could understand why a disfigured young girl would explore her sexuality through the safety of a telephone line. He'd spent a lot of time and money talking to Bliss, and he wanted to think that the relationship they'd been building was as special and beneficial to her as it was to him.

Gary knew a lot of women. He and Felicia had made a host of friends over the years, which was evidenced by the overflowing crowd of mourners at her funeral. But he could think of no one other than Bliss who fit the criteria that had been specified by his wife, and as he rode in the taxi toward a virtual stranger's home bearing over fifty thousand dollars' worth of his dead wife's jewelry, Gary hoped that he and his offerings would be warmly received.

There was nothing he wanted from Bliss other than what she'd already been giving him. Despite her physical appearance and her obvious embarrassment due to the early trauma and abuse she'd revealed during the telethon, Gary thought she was a wonderful, beautiful young lady. The kind of young lady who was highly deserving of the most beautiful of jewels. The kind of young lady that Gary and Felicia would have been proud to have had as their daughter.

Gary sighed and shifted the box in his lap. *Sixty-seven Third Avenue. Apartment 8G,* he mouthed the address silently.

Be with me. Gary uttered a silent supplication to his wife. *I'm just trying to go where you lead, baby. So be with me.*

For the first time ever, Bliss was outside of the Purple Room.

Dressed in a purple silk pantsuit trimmed in tiny gold sequins, her body had been oiled with jasmine extract and her hair was upswept with sparkling gold pins. She made her way past the Sick Room where Bertha reigned and into the kitchen using only the doorways and walls to brace herself.

Humming a sultry Nina Simone tune she'd once heard playing in Matthew's office, Bliss smiled as she checked the table setting one last time. She'd purchased the silverware online and learned the proper placement from Mannersinternational.com.

The heels on Bliss's purple shoes dragged along the linoleum as she leaned heavily on the table and poured herself a glass of wine. In just a few minutes Matthew would be walking through the door, and there were anticipatory ants jumping around in her tight purple pants. She wasn't cool enough to sit down.

Sipping the sweet liquid, Bliss inhaled and let her imagination run wild. What would Matthew's fantasy be? Would he crave it hot and nasty? A little freak on his menu to keep his battery juiced? Or was there something dark and hidden that he desired? Some throwback secret that turned him on by night but shamed him to no end by day?

Bliss giggled, the wine heating up her blood. It didn't matter what it took to get Matthew Yarbridge through the night. She was every woman. It was all in her. She could tip his bucket. Peel his banana. Choke his chicken. Wax his willie. Clean his clock. Pull his peter. Ring his bell. Rock his motherfucking *world*. She was Bliss. The freak of every man's dreams, and tonight Matthew Yarbridge was going to be the luckiest man in the world, because tonight he would have Beautiful Bliss all to himself.

The doorbell rang at exactly 5:00 PM and Bliss's heart

pounded twice in her chest as Matthew's name came to her lips. She had been sipping wine and grooving to some easy jazz sounds on the living room sofa, and even though her tipsy mind told her she should sprint toward the front door at the sound of the bell, her disabilities trumped the half bottle of wine she'd put away, so she shuffled along at her usual snail's pace.

"Easy, girl, easy," she told herself. "Let the man wait and anticipate." She had no desire to open the door looking like a sweaty freak anyway.

Turning the top lock first, then throwing the bolt on the bottom lock, Bliss opened the door wearing a dazzling smile.

"Chinese?"

Her smile fell. An Asian man she'd never seen before stood there with his arms full of take-out food from Ming Su Yung's.

"Oh," Bliss said, disappointed. She'd been concentrating so hard on Matthew that she'd forgotten all about the food. She looked at the mountain of bags piled in the cardboard box the man bore. Hyacinth usually dealt with the food deliveries. All Bertha usually did was spoon her own contents out the carton and eat.

"Can you bring it inside?" she asked. This guy looked a little bit on the old side for a delivery boy, and she wasn't thrilled about letting him in her house, but she couldn't carry all that food and walk at the same time, either.

He stood there for a second and Bliss figured they had a little language barrier going.

"Come." She gestured and raised her voice like that would make him understand her better. "Bring it inside."

Perhaps it was the wine, or maybe it was the sweet sounds of jazz flowing in from the living room, or maybe it was anticipation and the newfound freedom that Bliss was experiencing outside of the Purple Room, but her hips swayed a bit as she held on to the walls and led the Chinese man into the kitchen.

His face was blank and unreadable as he stepped into the small room behind her and Bliss wondered if he'd been in the country long enough to learn a word of English or whether he was straight off the boat.

"You can put everything over there on the counter," Bliss said, pointing and nodding toward a space she'd cleared near the dish rack. She repeated louder, "Over there."

Using the breakfront for leverage, Bliss shuffled herself around to retrieve an envelope from the drawer where the house money was kept. She thumbed through a stack of twenties and slid five off the top, and when she turned back around to pay him, the man was sitting at her table at the place setting she'd reserved for Matthew.

Bliss blinked. "What the hell are you doing?"

The man just stared at her. He was late fortyish and slender with sleek, oily hair. His slanted eyes were set wide apart and there was a mixture of curiosity and rapture on his face that made Bliss shiver.

"Excuse me?" Bliss held out the money. "How much do I owe you?"

"You remind me of my mother," he said softly.

"What?" Not only had this fool plopped his ass down at her table, he spoke perfect English.

"Don't be afraid, Bliss," he whispered, his eyes boring into hers. "Your skin . . . those scars . . . the suffering. I know you. I *know* you."

With her hand still on the breakfront drawer, Bliss couldn't believe her luck. Here she was stuck with a nutcase in her own damned kitchen and he was sitting between her and a big rack of knives.

"No, I don't think so," she said, trying to sound assertive. "You might have met my mother if you delivered food here before. Or maybe you met my boyfriend. He'll be here for dinner in a second, so why don't you just take your money and move on."

"No, Bliss," the man said, using her phone name for

the second time. "You don't have a boyfriend. You're a *virgin*, remember?"

Bliss went for the phone.

He was out of his seat before she was halfway there.

Bliss stared as he ripped the phone from the wall and walked calmly over to the window and tossed it out.

"W-w-who the fuck *are* you?"

"*You've never done this before*," the man mimicked in a singsong Chinese accent as he came back to the table. "Have you? Nineteen and you're still a virgin? I know it's your first time. I'll be gentle. What are you wearing? Is your hair blond? Are you pretty? Do you look like Angelina Jolie? Touch me! Put your hand on my chest and rub my nipples."

"*Cho!*" Bliss blurted.

The wine rushed to her head and her vision blurred.

"What are you doing here?" she cried. "How the hell did you find me?"

The Asian man shrugged. "Please do not be afraid, dear Bliss. I only want to protect you. I've waited my entire life to find a woman like you. You remind me of my mother," he said again. "Like you, she suffered greatly, Bliss. But like you, she was also beautiful. You're beautiful, Bliss. Beautiful."

And then he smiled.

CHAPTER 15

SHALL I wait for you, sir?"

Matthew Yarbridge shook his head as his driver held his door.

"No. I might be a while. I'll buzz you when I'm ready."

He strode into the building with long, sure steps. He was having dinner with Bertha tonight, but his thoughts were filled with his own daughter. Her health had been on the downslide recently, and although he still worked tirelessly on behalf of the causes he believed in, the main thrust of Matthew's energies had been concentrated on his child.

Just thinking about children brought Bertha back to mind. She was a lonely young thing and she'd always beer fixated on him. Matthew knew she was going through some sort of savior syndrome, and that all the flirting and sexual innuendos she threw at him were nothing but gratitude being expressed in the only way she knew how.

The lobby manager was wearing earplugs and holding an iPod, and he greeted Matthew with a warm wave. The foundation owned several apartments in the building and all staff members had been trained to recognize and respond to him as a VIP. Matthew rubbed his stomach as he waited for the elevator. He hadn't eaten since breakfast, and while spending time with Bertha was great, he was also hungry as heck.

When the elevator arrived, two elderly women got off and Matthew gave them both a smile. Brooklyn had been revitalized over the years, and this was still a pretty safe neighborhood where older residents could take a walk in the evenings if they wanted. There'd been a recent rash of elderly and disabled beatings citywide, and the police had cracked down on the perpetrators. Matthew was proud that he helped provide a safe place for the foundation's clients to live, which was why raising money was so important.

Matthew stepped into the elevator and pressed eight. He hummed along with the piped-in music and closed his eyes as the car ascended. He was tired and in no condition to fight off Bertha's advances, but it was definitely time to redraw a line for her. He might have looked young, but he was getting to be an old man and he had an old man's lifestyle. Bertha was still very young, and despite her physical limitations the world was wide open and anything was in her reach.

As her friend and her benefactor Matthew felt it was his place to tell her that. All this dreaming and hoping she was doing to get next to him was in vain. Bertha needed to find herself a young man who had a young heart and young dreams. Someone who could discover the world with her, then help her conquer it.

Matthew thrust his hands in his pants pockets and sighed. He leaned against the elevator wall and all at once the music stopped, the lights when out, and the elevator car lurched to a halt.

Third Avenue was lit up as Lattrell sauntered down the sidewalk sticking close to the buildings. He'd hopped out of his limo a few blocks down and pulled his hoodie over his face so he wouldn't be recognized. New York was a place that Lattrell had always loved, and no other borough was hotter than Brooklyn.

His boy Twenty had put in some damn good work

and Lattrell had memorized the address he was looking for: *67 Third Avenue.* Five minutes later he was standing outside the building trying to look like he belonged there. Lattrell checked out the kind of people who came in and out of the building. Most were either old, white, or both, and there was also a guy checking people out in the lobby so he knew he wouldn't be able to slide in. He was leaning against the building and working on a plan when a Papa John's delivery car pulled up to the curb.

A skinny white dude got out holding two boxes of pizza and Lattrell sprang into action.

"Damn, man, what took you so long?" He towered over the kid, who looked like he wanted to drop the pizza and run. "Here." Lattrell dug in his pocket and pulled out two twenties. "Got my aunt upstairs all hungry and you out here bullshitting around."

Lattrell walked into the building holding the pizzas on top of his shoulder, hoping like hell he looked like a pizza man. The guy in uniform was jamming to some sounds. He nodded and Lattrell nodded right back, and pressed the button for the elevator and waited.

"Might be a minute," the guy called out loudly behind him. Lattrell could tell the dude's music was blasting by the way he was yelling. "It hasn't been down in a while. Somebody must be up there holding it."

Lattrell nodded, not bothering to answer. Dude was jamming and he wouldn't have heard him anyway. Ducking his head, Lattrell headed toward the stairwell, holding the pizza boxes firmly in his hands.

The stairwell door had just closed behind Lattrell when a young, muscular white man walked into the building wearing an electrician's tool belt.

"It's broken," the lobby manager yelled out, bopping to the beat as the blond-haired man headed toward the elevator.

The white man waved his arm in thanks, then shifted his stride left and headed in the direction of the stairs. He whistled as he jogged easily up the steps, an assortment of metal tools clanking at his waist. He rounded the steps on the seventh floor and just ahead of him he saw a tall black man carrying a stack of pizza boxes. Jim followed him and was surprised when the young man exited the stairwell on the next floor.

Jim trailed the young black man out of the exit. The kid turned down the hall to the right and Jim hung back, waiting to see which apartment the thuggish-looking guy was delivering to.

Moments later Jim heard him knocking on a door

"Papa John's!" the kid called loudly.

Jim listened as a door opened and an older man's voice floated into the hall.

"Go away. We didn't order any pizza."

"Look, man," the black guy said, "don't give me no shit. I need to see the lady who lives here. I need to see *Bliss*."

"Bliss doesn't want to see you. I had her first. She only wants to see *me*."

At the sound of her name, Jim went cold.

He peered around the corner and watched as the black kid had an exchange with a small Asian man who was dressed in a white smock.

Something big clicked in Jim's brain. A lesser man might have hesitated, but in his state of rage none of the stereotypes fazed him. He strode around the corner quickly, pulling a construction wrench from his tool belt as he moved. With his eyes straight ahead, he took two steps past the men, then whirled around and swung the wrench in a high arc.

Blood gushed from the top of Lattrell's head, irrigating his braids in a crimson stream. The Papa John's pizzas slid from his grip and Lattrell hit the ground unconscious and lay sprawled in the doorway in a tangled heap.

Cho's eyes grew wide and he stumbled backward in ~ar.

"No!" he cried. "Who are you? Get away from here!"

Gripping his bloody wrench, Jim stood on top of Lattrell's prone body, then advanced deeper into the apartment.

And making her way out of the kitchen, Bliss screamed.

Bliss was too through.

Her first time out of the Purple Room and she'd stepped into a friggin' nightmare.

Either that half a bottle of wine had her tripping, or Bliss needed to wake her ass up because she knew this just had to be a bad dream. One minute she'd been sipping wine and feeling frisky, and the next thing she knew some crazy Chinese client who needed to fuck a virginal Angelina Jolie three times a week was sitting at her kitchen table.

Bliss wanted to scream but her mouth was too damned dry. Instead she had sat there listening as Cho gave her a raging history lesson about the bombing of Hiroshima and how its victims deserved reparations, protection, and respect from their evil American enemies.

Cho was twisted, that was for real. And somehow he had twisted her up with the loving memory of his dead mother.

"You don't really know me," Bliss insisted. "Look at me. I'm *not* Angelina Jolie. Can't you see that? And I'm not your mother, either."

"But you're beautiful. You're someone who makes me want to shield you from the world. I'd like to keep you someplace safe, someplace where nobody ever stared at you and pointed again, where nobody ever made you feel ashamed of who you are."

He scared the shit out of Bliss. She took him for the type who would lock her ass in an underground dungeon and keep her down there for her own good.

"Look, Cho. None of what you think about me is real. It's all just a fantasy! I'm happy with my life! I'm—"

Someone knocked at the door, startling them both.

"Matthew," Bliss whispered.

She glanced at Cho, who had a strange look in his eyes.

"You'd better let me answer that. He knows I'm here and if I don't answer he'll come back with the police."

Cho stood. "No." He pointed at a chair. "Sit down. I'll answer it."

Bliss sat at the table as he walked past her out of the

kitchen and strode down her short hall. Nothing ever shocked her more than when she heard someone yell, "Papa John's!" outside her door.

What the hell? she thought as she gripped the edges of her chair. She pulled herself to her feet as her front door was opened.

"Go away. We didn't order any pizza."

"Look man, don't give me no shit. I need to see the lady who lives here. I need to see *Bliss.*"

"Bliss doesn't want to see you. I had her first. She only wants to see *me.*"

Bliss had almost passed out at the sound of her name. She knew that voice. She'd gotten his CD in the mail and had been listening to it for most of the morning.

She shuffled toward the doorway. How in the hell Lattrell "La-Rule" came to be standing outside her door was anybody's guess, but Bliss would rather take her chances with a homo thug than with that crazy-ass Cho any day of the week.

The two men were going back and forth as Bliss gripped the walls and rounded the corner. She was just opening her mouth to scream Lattrell's name when out of nowhere a hulking white man stepped into view and swung something over his head, dropping Lattrell to the ground like a sack of rocks.

Cho backpedaled toward her, trying to get away.

"No!" he cried. "Who are you? Get away from here!"

The white man stepped right on Lattrell as he walked into Bliss's apartment, and standing in the doorway of her kitchen, all she could do was scream.

CHAPTER 16

CHO backed down the hall with his fingertips brushing the walls. All he wanted to do was go back to his restaurant and mind his own business. Whatever chaos Bliss was involved in was none of his concern. With so many men running through her apartment he had obviously been very wrong about her. She was no virgin. She wasn't even beautiful! And right now, his life was in danger as an armed stranger advanced on him with menace in his eyes.

"Sir," Cho pleaded, his Asian accent suddenly thick, "I do not know this woman, sir. I am merely a delivery-man. I am just bringing your dinner, sir. Please. Allow me to exit the apartment, sir, and you may do with h as you please."

If Bliss's feet had been right she would have kicked Cho's little ass! So much for all that protecting and shielding and safeguarding shit. Bliss didn't know *who* the fuck the big bad wolf coming down her hall was, but Chicken Little Cho was ready to fling her straight into his jaws!

"You dirty black hooker," the white man growled. He reached down and dragged Lattrell into the apartment by his hood, allowing the door to slam closed.

There was murder in the man's eyes. He was looking at Bliss, but he reached out and snatched Cho up like the little man weighed less than fifty pounds and lifted him off his feet as he squeezed his neck.

Bliss screamed again as the little man's feet kicked wildly in the air. Cho fought back hard, punching and flailing around, trying to save his own life. He butted his head into the white man's nose, stunning him long enough to break his neck hold. But the white man got him in the clutch again, and this time they went down on the floor and scuffled.

There was no way the little Asian man could win. The life was being choked out of him and his movements were growing more and more feeble when out of ɔwhere Lattrell staggered to his feet and threw himself ɔp of the white man's back.

"Oh my God!" Bliss hollered. "Kick his ass, Lattrell! Kick his ass!!"

All she could do was lean against the wall as Lattrell and the white man went at it. This one was a much fairer fight, with the white man taking just as many blows as he threw. Lattrell was a buff-ass something, and even though he was a bottom boy he straddled Jim's back and threw killer punches with precision.

Bliss cheered him on. She was yelling and screaming out instructions like he was a prizefighter and she was his corner man, when her front door swung open a crack and a breathless voice called out.

"Is everything all right in there?" The voice was hesitant, but it was also very familiar. "I was going to ring the bell but I heard a lot of noise . . . I just wanted to make sure that Bliss was okay . . ."

Bliss watched as a middle-aged black man stepped partway into her foyer. He was breathing hard and carrying a box in his arms. She placed the voice way before she placed the face. She'd sang to him on many nights but she'd only seen him once.

"Gary!" she screamed. "Help us! Help us! *Help*!!!"

For an older man who had just walked up eight flights of stairs, Gary reacted damned fast. Stepping fully into the apartment, he lifted the heavy jewelry bo high in the air and brought it down with every ounce of his strength.

For the second time that evening, Lattrell got clocked. He'd never even seen it coming. The packed metal jewelry case caught him flush on his head and sent him spiraling right back into darkness.

"Oh *no!*" Bliss cried. "Not *him!*"

With the young thug slumped halfway off his back, Jim rolled over and struggled to his feet. He glared at the old black man who stood in the doorway looking tired and confused. Jim didn't know who he was, but he didn't care who he had to take down to get next to the whore. He wasn't leaving until the piece of black trash who had stolen his future was dead.

Jim took a step toward the old man, who quickly raised his arms in self-defense.

"Please . . . no . . ."

Jim glanced over his shoulder and saw that Bliss was crying and trembling. She was a dreadful-looking thing. Twisted and ugly. Not pretty, slender, or white. He shuddered in revulsion and spoke to her briefly.

"Pizza . . . Chinese food . . . how many times do I have to tell you, dear, that you look like what you eat." Jim turned his lips down and grimaced. "Well, you must eat ⁻traight out of the toilet, Bliss, because you look like shit."

• • •

Dinner was the last thing on Matthew's mind as the security team freed him from the hot elevator. He'd been stuck inside for the past fifteen minutes, and for a man who took pride in staying calm, his temper was just about off the charts.

There was never an excuse for incompetence as far as he was concerned, and the first order of business the next morning would be to make sure that the lobby manager was fired. As soon as he realized he was trapped, the first call Matthew had made was to the number listed inside the elevator for the lobby manager on duty. That idiot hadn't answered and Matthew remembered seeing him wearing earplugs and holding an iPod when he'd come in. The second call had been to his driver, who had already headed toward Manhattan and was stuck in traffic going toward the Brooklyn Bridge.

Matthew had also tried Bertha's number, and to his surprise she hadn't answered, either. It had taken a lot of banging and stomping and a little old lady who needed to get downstairs and walk her poodle in order to get anybody's attention. Thankfully, she'd located the security team, which was able to flip an emergency switch and get the doors opened. They were a capable your team of African-American men and had been very respectful and apologetic when they arrived to find Matthew stuck between the fourth and fifth floors.

"Don't worry, sir," one of the young men had called out. "We'll have the door open in just a second."

And seconds later, it was open. Matthew had stood back as the young guards hoisted themselves up into the stifling car one at a time.

"Careful now," he warned. He'd heard of enough people falling down elevator shafts to last a lifetime. "Get a good grip, you hear?"

Both men climbed inside easily and Matthew breathed a sigh of relief.

"I could have just as soon jumped down, you know," he told them. Matthew was rock hard and extremely fit for his age, and besides, he wasn't sure he trusted the elevator to take him up three more flights. "I'm only going to the eighth floor. I probably should have walked from the beginning."

"No problem," the second guard reassured him. He pressed the button for eight on the console and smiled. "We'll ride up with you and then take another look at the sensor and see if there's anything else we need to do."

Matthew was impressed with the courtesy and

bearing of the two young men. He could use black men like these at the foundation. He'd given each of them one of his business cards and invited them to call him, and now, as he wiped perspiration from his brow and walked briskly toward Bertha's apartment, he wasn't even hungry anymore and wished he had stayed home and eaten a sandwich.

He was halfway down the hall when he heard all the ruckus.

It sounded like bodies were being flung up against a wall, and a woman was crying and begging for help. Matthew slowed his steps and moved cautiously. What was going on? Perhaps more of that senior abuse he'd read about?

Bertha's apartment was the first door on the left, and the sounds were too near to be coming from anywhere further down the hall. Seconds later he knew it was her. He could hear her voice clearly, wailing and terrified. Matthew hesitated only for a second. He reached for his cell phone, then realized there was no time to call for help. Pushing open the door he was stunned by the sight that greeted him.

Blood was on the foyer's floor and there were bodies lying everywhere. A black guy was on his stomach, an Asian guy lay on his back. A large white man was on his knees, and his hands were gripping the neck of a much smaller person. Matthew could only stand there. It all seemed surreal because the man being choked looked a lot like his fraternity brother and good friend Gary Browning, but that was impossible.

Or so he thought.

"Matthew, *help!*" Bertha screamed. "He's killing him! He's killing *Gary!*"

A body moves on its own when it needs to. The brain needn't tell it a damn thing. It just does what it knows has to be done.

With lightning speed, Matthew got down on the man's level. He slid both his arms under the white man's armpits and then quickly interlaced his fingers behind the man's neck. Using every bit of his considerable strength, he pressed the man's neck forward, applying enough force to crack his spine and trapping him in a crippling full nelson.

The man released Gary and struggled. He flailed his arms backward, yanking the right side of Matthew's glasses and knocking them from his nose.

Gary rolled over, coughing, but had the presence of mind to help. He snatched the remaining tools from the man's belt and flung them down the hall.

The man gasped in rage and bent forward at the

waist, but Matthew pressed on, bending his neck at an excruciating angle and feeling strong enough to snap it clean through.

"Get to the door!" Matthew grunted to Bertha. "There are security guards right near the elevator! Call to them from the door!"

It was the journey of a lifetime as Bertha held on to the walls and maneuvered around the bodies that were stretched out on her floor. She was trembling from head to toe as she neared the two struggling men. She could feel the evil and the rage radiating from Jim Burgess, and she froze several feet away from him, too terrified to get any closer.

"Go, Bertha," Matthew gasped. The younger man was weaker but still fighting. "I've got him, baby. Just trust me. I won't let him go."

Moments later Bertha had opened the door and was on her knees with her calls for help echoing loudly down the hall. Matthew felt a sense of blessed relief as footsteps pounded toward the apartment and help came rushing through the door.

"We've got him, Mr. Yarbridge," the same young man who had just freed Matthew from the elevator said. The name BRADLEY was on his jacket. "You can let him go now, sir. We've got him."

Matthew looked up, exhausted and with grateful eyes. "You sure? He's strong, now. You sure you can handle him?"

The security guard unsheathed his nightstick.

"Oh, yeah. Let him go. Let's see if he can handle me."

Matthew unlaced his aching fingers and sat back on the floor. He looked over at his friend Gary, then reached out to pat his leg.

"Are you okay, old man?"

Rubbing his throat, Gary coughed a bit, then nodded.

"Bertha!" Matthew called as the security guards handcuffed the young white man he'd nearly put to sleep. "Are you okay, dear?"

"Yes." She sniffed, still on her knees by the door. "I'm okay."

"Good," Matthew said, scooting back against the wall and pushing himself to his feet. "Because you can forget about me *and* dinner, darling. Find somebody your own damn age. This is too much drama for me."

CHAPTER 17

IN the months that had passed since Beautiful Bliss died and her 1-900 hard-core phone sex line was shut down, a lot had changed in the world. Wars had been waged, new planets had been discovered, an entire species of animal life had gone extinct, and Bertha Sampson had been reborn.

Today, Bertha sat behind the large receptionist's desk at the Yarbridge Foundation, grateful for the brief lull in the ringing phone lines. She'd spent the morning soliciting sponsorship and donations for the foundation, using her beguiling voice and outgoing phone personality to form relationships and build alliances with individuals and corporations that could provide the necessary capital and influence to help further the foundation's mission to aid physically disabled children and adults nationwide.

Bertha loved her new job, but being out freely in the world was still a little strange for her, and the past three months had been a series of exciting new experiences and revelations, one right after the next.

For a person who was self-taught and so well read, there was a lot that Bertha discovered she didn't know. Living her life confined within the walls of 67 Third Avenue didn't exactly qualify her as a globetrotter, and no matter how many Internet searches one conducted or how many professional articles one read, there was only so much knowledge that could be gained without the benefit of healthy human interactions.

Coming out of her shell and exploring the outside world required more of Bertha than simply getting dressed and putting on a jacket and allowing Hyacinth to wheel her outside. She had to come clean first and open herself up to the same things that able-bodied people faced outside their doors on a daily basis.

Humanity.

"You was doing *what* in that room?" Hyacinth had asked in disbelief. "Bertha Jean Sampson!"

Hyacinth might not have approved of what had

gone on in the Purple Room, but she couldn't make Bertha feel bad about it. Bliss had lived inside of her for a reason. There were some serious issues that Bertha had gotten to explore through her sexy alter ego. Bliss had fulfilled a buried need to exploit her mind and her repressed creativity, because deep inside Bertha was highly sexual but hugely ashamed of her disfigured body.

But what Bliss had done in the Purple Room wasn't anything that women across the world didn't do every day. Duping men, faking orgasms, lulling them with voices and visual stimulation that existed solely in their minds. But it was *not* all a game, she now realized. It was intimate. It *was* really sex. And, as Bertha had learned on a fright-filled night in her very own kitchen, there was no complete anonymity. There was always the possibility of a very real connection.

Of course, everyone involved had been there for their own selfish reasons. Every one of them had desired and fantasized about the very thing they couldn't have. Whether it was disgust for an ethnic group, the repression of one's true sexuality, a repulsion brought on by a traumatic experience or, as in Gary's case, just plain old grief and loneliness, everyone was seeking their own humanity in someone else. They were looking to plug in someplace, to cross their fantasies into someone else's realities. Without consequences. Without judgment.

Cho had come from a proud family of immigrants who couldn't stand white folks. Talk about reverse racism? The Yungs had never gotten over the horrors inflicted by the bombing in Hiroshima, and Cho and his brothers had been taught to hate Americans because of their mother's suffering. But what about all the Americans who had died during the Japanese bombing of Pearl Harbor? Bertha had asked him that question as he'd sat raging at her kitchen table. Weren't the Japanese just as liable for those families' loss and pain? And if it wasn't for the kindly white American folks who had adopted Cho's mother, the Yung family might never have had the opportunity to come to this country and build an empire off the economic suffering of another downtrodden and misaligned ethnic group. It was a dog-eat-dog world out there. Everybody had bloody fur on their lips.

Lattrell's situation had been a lot more complicated. His conflictions ran deep and hit him in his heart and in his spirit. After battling for his life inside Bertha's apartment, La-Rule had given up his public lifestyle. It was too damned much. All the lying and the scheming, all the careful watching of his every action, his every mannerism, just to make sure there was nothing about him that even remotely hinted at his true self—it was just too much.

"I'm done rapping," he'd told Bertha. He'd spent two nights in the hospital with a severe concussion, and one of the first things he'd done when he was released was respond to the message of concern that Bertha had left on his cell phone. "Game over. It's time to give it up," he said sadly. "My heart just ain't in it no more."

Bertha wasn't really surprised. She knew his deepest secrets, and all that flashy jewelry and stage bravado and hard-core gangsta rap might have fooled most people, but when you've had a front-row seat in somebody's sexual fantasies it was pretty hard to fool them.

"What's so bad about being gay?" Bertha had asked Lattrell. She didn't bother to ask him if he *was* gay. There was no doubt that he was as gay as they came, and all that imaginary back door action he'd been giving up to Neck was proof of that.

"I used to think it was the worst thing in the world," Lattrell confessed. "My father's a Southern preacher, so I was raised to think that way. But I'm tired of being what everybody else wants me to be, Bertha. I'm done with all the fake bullshit, with all the frontin' and scheming and working hard to make everybody think I'm just like them. I can't be who my father wants me to be. I can't be my brothers. I'm his son too, Bertha. I'm a Johnson man, just like the rest of them. But I'm still *me*. And me is all I can be."

The last time Bertha heard from Lattrell he had joined a church in Atlanta that was nondenominational and open to the masses, no matter who or what they were. He'd emailed to tell her that he was singing in the choir and enjoying the fellowship but was still struggling to reconcile his faith with his sexuality, but he felt he was making progress.

Which was not something that everyone was willing or able to do. Sally Godfrey had ceased being a client well before the floor dropped out from under Bliss's feet, but that didn't mean her issues had been resolved. Sally was still living behind her façade of wedded bliss. Bertha wasn't sure if Sally was totally gay, but she was definitely bisexual and had a dark, kinky side of her sexuality that she would probably never reveal to her husband. Bertha wondered if Sally had found herself another imaginary bottom bitch to stomp on her nipples and spank her inner thighs, but once their anonymity was breached they never discussed sex or their hot S & M trysts together again.

But true to her word, Sally had been doing some fine work on Bertha's behalf and had dug up other cases where disabled people had successfully sued and recovered damages for the horrible effects of Gulf War syndrome.

Bertha had been shocked speechless when Sally sat down with her to go through some precedent-setting cases. If Bertha thought her life had been rough, there were others out there who were suffering far worse dis-figurements and disabilities than she had ever imagined. And once she had committed herself to Bertha's case, Sally was relentless. She went after the government with the same tenacity that she had attacked every opponent she had ever stared down. She was suing the military and Veterans Administration for back payment of full disability compensation for Bertha, retroactive from birth until the age of twenty-three, and there was little doubt in Bertha's mind that with Sally on her case it was only a matter of time until she received every dime of what she was due.

And speaking of what was due, the very best thing that had come out of all this had been the relationship that Bertha had developed with Gary.

"Set it up," he'd told her just a few days earlier, and Bertha had done just that.

"Go ahead," Gary said. "Call it."

Bertha had chuckled. She called it the same way every time.

"Onyx before ivory. I'm black."

Gary had given her his usual response.

"Good choice. For tonight, I'm white."

All that teacher-student mess had long gone out the window. They played cutthroat chess these days, and it was nothing like the online games they used to play back when Bertha still had her 1-900 line. For one thing, they no longer played over the phone and the Internet. These days Gary came to Bertha's apartment twice a week, and while Bertha had grown to love the old man like the father she'd never had, that didn't stop her from beating him mercilessly if he slipped up and left his queen hanging out in the breeze.

"You're almost a genius," he told her, shaking his head at the series of intellectual moves she made on the board. "Almost," he said, sneaking up on her queen from a narrow pathway that Bertha hadn't anticipated and had neglected to protect.

"Checkmate." Gary laughed, shaking his head at the stunned look of disappointment on Bertha's face. "Don't be mad, Bertha. You've got a damn good read on the board, but nobody can predict every little thing that might be coming toward them. You're getting better every day, though. Pretty soon I won't be able to do much with you."

Bertha didn't know what she would have done without Gary, though. There hadn't been even a hint of awkwardness in transitioning their relationship from the telephone to real life. Probably because it had always been pure and built upon friendship and respect, things that bound them at the heart.

"My 1-900 number is being shut down," Bertha had told him shortly after all the chaos went down in her apartment on that crazy night. She couldn't figure out why the hell he had shown up at her door lugging a heavy box of expensive jewelry, and Gary couldn't apologize enough for cold-cocking Lattrell with the last of his wife's worldly possessions.

"I can explain everything," he'd promised as the paramedics were wheeling him down the hall and toward the elevator. "I promise you, Bertha. I know it looks crazy, but I had a damn good reason for coming here tonight."

Later, when things had calmed down, Gary shared his story with Bertha. He told her about his wife's letters, and about her instructions to rid his life of all reminders of her, except those that he carried in his heart.

"Felicia loved fine jewelry. She spent a lot of time picking out pieces that really spoke to her. She believed each piece of jewelry held the essence of the person who made it, and she swore she could feel their emotions and their auras when she wore their work on her body.

"Felicia's first letter was so hard for me to read. It was almost like she wanted me to forget her right away. To just wipe away all traces of her like she had never existed, like what we'd had for all those years had never existed. She demanded that I get rid of all her possessions. Some things she wanted to be given to someone specific, some things she wanted thrown away, and other things she left for me to decide where they should go.

"Her jewelry, though . . . she told me to give her jewelry to someone special . . . someone I thought would remind me of the beauty of our love. And that's when I thought of you, Bertha. That's why I was at your apartment that night. Felicia and I had a lot of friends. We traveled the world and met a lot of people and formed a lot of good relationships. But out of everyone I knew, the only person I could imagine honoring with my wife's jewelry was you."

Bertha had been more than honored. If she lived to be a hundred she would probably never have afforded the kind of elegant and stylish jewelry that Felicia Browning had collected during her lifetime, but she was thankful for the gift and made sure she wore something of Felicia's whenever Gary came by to play chess.

One thing had changed between her and Gary, though. Bertha no longer sang "Lovin' You" to him anymore. It seemed that Gary was beginning to accept that Felicia, like Minnie, was gone. That song was for another time and another place. Just one more thing that he would treasure in the depths of his heart.

"Do you know that song about thanking the Holy Father for shining his light on thee?" Gary had asked one afternoon. Bertha had been confused until he hummed a slightly familiar tune, even though it was way off-key.

"Oh," she said grinning. "You're talking about 'I Wanna Thank You' by Alicia Meyers, right?" Bertha shook her head. Alicia Meyers had put such a hurting on that song that it was a hit on both gospel and R & B charts.

"But she's singing thank you Heavenly Father, not Holy Father," she corrected him gently. "And it's for 'shining your light on *me*,' not on thee."

Gary nodded. "Yeah, that's it, that's it. You think you can you sing that one for me?"

Bertha had nodded as Gary smiled. It was a good song. She remembered it from those old days on the road with Aunt Lurene and Uncle Long.

She cleared her throat and prepared to hit those beautiful notes the same way Alicia used to hit them. *"I wanna thank you . . . Heavenly Father. . . ."*

But not everybody had emerged from the drama unscathed and thanking the Lord. There had been murderous intent in Jim Burgess's heart that could have had fatal consequences, and that meant some mean pipers still had to be paid. If it wasn't for Cho, Lattrell, Gary, and Matthew, Jim Burgess would have put her in the morgue that night, Bertha was sure of it. To this day she couldn't figure out exactly what she'd done to piss her ex-client off so bad that the sight of her filled him with enough rage to want her dead, but it didn't matter. Crazy didn't have to make sense, and Jim was one of those brilliantly crazy nuts.

He'd bust up in her apartment like a maniac, packing a knife, some rope, and a tool belt full of lethal weapons, and he didn't give a damn who he had to stab, tie up, or bludgeon to get his hands on Bertha; he meant to lay her ass out cold. Jim had been arrested and charged with attempted murder, breaking and entering, and assault with a deadly weapon, and as they led him out of the courtroom after his hearing he'd fought the court officers and spit at Bertha and screamed, "Don't you look at me, you diseased black bitch! I never fucked you! I never touched your filthy black ass!"

The prosecutor was sure of a conviction and said Jim would probably never get out of prison, and Bertha hoped they'd put his ass so far under the jail that he'd need a telescope to see the sun.

But with everybody else coming to grips with their issues and moving on with their lives, where did that leave Bertha? In a way, she was a client too. She'd become a consumable. The bare bones left behind when everybody else's fantasies were stripped away. She had participated in the madness and orchestrated her own fantasies built around Matthew Yarbridge, the man who had saved her, a man she couldn't possibly have.

"Almost ready?"

Bertha looked up and smiled. It was lunchtime and Deon Bradley was a gorgeous piece of man. His dark brown skin and dimpled chin got her worked up in all the right places. He'd been one of the security guards who had come to her rescue the night one of Bliss's clients had almost become Bertha's killer. Matthew had hired Deon and his coworker to work in program management at the foundation, and Bertha had gotten her corporate sponsorship position with the foundation a few weeks later.

Bertha and Deon had been eating lunch and hanging out heavy for a couple of months, just getting to know each other. He'd invited her to his mother's house for dinner a few times and Bertha had met his sisters and his aunts and everybody had treated her like she was as able-bodied as anyone else. They'd pulled her wheelchair up to the kitchen table and taught her how to play bid whist, and when Deon's dad played dirty and reneged her out of her books, they all laughed and told Bertha she could consider herself family because Pops would never cheat a guest.

Hyacinth had cautioned Bertha to take her time with Deon since he was her first boyfriend and all, but so far, what Bertha saw in him she really, really liked. And, since Deon couldn't stop calling and visiting after actually seeing the *real* her, Bertha guessed he must have really liked her too.

And now he stood next to her wanting to know if she was ready to roll.

"I'm always ready," Bertha laughed as he gripped the handles of her wheelchair and steered her toward the elevator.

"Where are we eating?" he asked. "It's your turn to pick."

"Umm . . ." Bertha twirled her scarf in her hand. Something delicious was stirring between her legs and she wasn't even thinking about no lunch. The way Deon's smile flashed and his muscles bulged? Shit, to hell with Hyacinth and taking all that damn time! It had been three months. Not three hours or three weeks. Three months. That was time enough.

"I'm not really all that hungry," Bertha cooed melodically as they rode downstairs in the elevator. "Maybe we can grab a hero and just sit outside in the park and talk or something."

A warm breeze blew past as they exited the building, taking with it all of Bertha's inhibitions.

"Hey, D," she said slying, glancing at him over her shoulder.

Lord, the man was fine.

Her voice dipped sweetly down into the Bliss zone.

"Did I ever tell you about my Purple Room?"

"Your Purple Room?" He looked amused.

"Nah, never heard of it."

Bertha giggled. The 1-900 phone line had been disconnected months ago but the room was still the sexiest little playpen on the planet.

"Oooh-oooh, *Deon*! Has a sistah got a story for you! Wait till I tell you about my Purple Room . . ."